"Domenico, we ar **pick up where we** **has happened. We** **Rae stammered.**

"Nor would I want to. I'm not talking about us resuming our married life, Rae," he clarified with a sharp edge of impatience to his words. "The idea of that is as offensive to me as it apparently is to you. I'm talking about *pretending*. Putting on a blissfully happy show. I'm confident the pretense won't be too arduous for you. After all, you did spend considerably longer than six months pretending to be a devoted, happy wife."

"And just how many remarks like that would I be expected to put up with in our joyous reunion?" Rae queried with a thunderous flash of her blue eyes.

"The truth is painful, Rae, isn't it? But worry not, our contact over the six months will be limited. Of course, in public we'll need to present a deliriously in-love front, and there will need to be a fair amount of public events, but in private we won't need to spend any time together at all..."

Rosie Maxwell has dreamed of being a writer since she was a little girl. Never happier than when she is lost in her own imagination, she is delighted that she finally has a legitimate reason to spend hours every day dreaming about handsome heroes and glamorous locations. In her spare time, she loves reading—everything from fiction to history to fashion and doing yoga. She currently lives in the North West of England.

Billionaire's Runaway Wife

ROSIE MAXWELL

HARLEQUIN

PRESENTS

HARLEQUIN®
PRESENTS™

Recycling programs
for this product may
not exist in your area.

ISBN-13: 978-1-335-59357-3

Billionaire's Runaway Wife

Harlequin Enterprises ULC
22 Adelaide St. West, 41st Floor
Toronto, Ontario M5H 4E3, Canada
www.Harlequin.com

Printed in Lithuania

MIX
Paper | Supporting
responsible forestry
FSC® C021394

Billionaire's
Runaway Wife

For my brother and sister-in-law, and my
two adorable nieces—with all my love xx

CHAPTER ONE

DOMENICO RICCI WAS in pain. His body was heavy with it, as if his bones had been lined with lead. Even the simple act of drawing in a breath was an effort, causing his chest to burn and his stomach muscles to sharply contract.

Grief, he thought disdainfully. It had always been his considered point of view that those who cited the crippling effects of grief were simply too weak to contend with the realities of life. Death was, after all, inevitable. A basic fact of life. It was far better to celebrate a person than wallow in mournful and distressed emotion upon their passing.

But now it was his adored aunt Elena who had departed the world and all Domenico could feel was the burden of sorrow. Even the sight of his beloved Venice—home since his scandalous and uncelebrated birth—in the mauve and indigo shadows of the approaching evening offered little comfort.

In spite of Elena's advanced age, he hadn't been prepared for it. For the loss of the only woman who had never rejected him and who had spent her life guiding and encouraging him. The woman who had given him a home and the embrace of a family when those who should have loved and cared for him had been set on deserting him to a crueller fate. And now she was gone.

Just like all those other people in his life, Elena had left him too.

In the faint reflection in the window Domenico watched his lips firm and lines of strain stream from the corners of his mouth as his meandering thoughts forced him to relive the rejections and desertions he had suffered over the years, beginning with his birth family and ending with his wife, Rae.

Rae.

His big body clenched as he thought of her, with her heart-shaped face, her tumble of chestnut hair and eyes so startlingly, beautifully blue they could penetrate even the coldest soul, compelling Domenico to raise the glass cradled between his fingers to his lips and numb the sudden sharp pinch of bitter feeling with a long swallow of the bright amber liquid. Out of all the women who had inflicted a scar, Rae had cut him the deepest. Because he had *chosen* her. He had invited her into his life, placed a ring on her finger and made a binding vow, and she had walked out on him. That desertion burned him far more than anything he had endured from his blood relatives.

Which made it all the more inexplicable that in his moment of sadness it was her comforting touch he craved. That out of all the mourners currently in his palazzo, hers was the only face he wanted to see, only she hadn't bothered to come and pay her respects…

Domenico raised the glass to his lips again, castigating his melancholic mood for turning him into a sentimental fool. Of course she hadn't come! Rae had left him. Rejected him. She hadn't even had the decency to tell him that she was unhappy in their marriage. Hadn't offered him the chance to fix whatever it was that was making her unhappy. She'd simply walked out of the door one day and left him to find the pathetic one-sentence note she had deigned to write to explain her sudden absence.

She was the last person deserving of room in his thoughts. The very last woman he should desire. If he needed comfort, there were countless others he could turn to, women who would appreciate him and be happy to share his bed. Because that was all that would be on offer. A night. An encounter. Never again would he open up his life to another soulless, treacherous female.

The floorboard behind him creaked in a way that told him someone was outside the door to his third-floor private study and then he heard the soft squeak of his partially closed door being nudged open. He remained still. Those who knew him knew better than to disturb him, which meant it was a stranger, someone seeking something he was probably in no mood to give. A reporter possibly, looking for a quote about Elena's passing, or some grossly nosy individual…

But then the skin on the back of his neck prickled, and his nose caught a light, barely-there scent and in defiance of the command issued straight from his brain, his heart missed a beat.

And he knew it was her.

* * *

'Domenico?'

Saying his name felt strange. After such a long period of not saying it, of determinedly keeping him out of her mind, it sent a quiver through Rae Dunbar's blood.

And as for laying eyes on him for the first time in months…

Her view was only of his rear as he faced away from her, his attention fixed on the timeless elegance and twilight romance of the city that rose from the water beyond the window, but with his strong back and shoulders so broad that they threatened to bust the seams of every item of clothing he wore, he was still magnificent to behold. So magnificent that her throat was suddenly sandpaper dry and it felt as if a swarm of butterflies had been unleashed in her chest.

Not that she had expected him to have changed, to suddenly have become lesser than the Adonis it was widely agreed he was, but Rae had hoped, quite ardently, that his effect on her would have lessened. Preferably to nothing at all. But with that single initial glance, it was painfully clear that wasn't the case.

'So you have bothered to show up. Late though you are,' he said, a visible surge of tension making the lines of his solid body even more distinct. Beneath the tailored black shirt he wore, Rae could make out the sharp definition of his powerful back muscles—muscles she had never tired of stroking her hands over—and without warning the need to feel his hot, smooth skin beneath her hands gushed through her veins, a torrent of helpless, burning longing.

'I know. I'm sorry,' Rae stammered, having to push past that overpowering compulsion to touch him in order to locate her voice. 'I've been trying to get here for days, ever since I read about Elena's passing, but an arctic storm was sat right over us. All trains and flights were cancelled. They only resumed today and I made sure that I was on the first plane out.'

The words raced out of her mouth and into one another in her haste to explain and exonerate herself of the aggravation he'd made no attempt to mask.

'I'm surprised you tried so hard.'

'I wanted to be here,' Rae responded immediately. 'To say goodbye to Elena and pay my respects to her—the wonderful woman she was.' Her words caught as she was pierced again by guilt over how long it had been since she'd seen or spoken to the older woman. And now it was too late. 'If I'd known she was ill...'

Domenico spun around, his face set in a thousand furious shadows. 'And how would you have known that, Rae? Given that you walked out on this family.'

'Please, Domenico,' Rae said, feeling his anger slam into her and almost knock her sideways, but after leaving him the way she had, she knew she deserved it. 'I didn't come here to argue.'

'Why come at all?' he demanded, some untethered emotion leaping dangerously in his darkened gaze as his stare closed around her. His fury only sharpened the chiselled planes of his face, making him more striking, and the dryness of Rae's throat intensified to an almost painful degree. 'You were under no obligation to, you made sure of that.'

'I told you.' Rae strove to keep her voice steady as she was treated to the full brutally masculine force of him. Six foot five, powerful shoulders, wide chest, jaw as sharp as a blade, aristocratic nose and eyes the shade of polished mahogany sat beneath thick, expressive brows. Looking at Domenico, no one could deny he'd been born to be a leader of men. In another time he would have been a warrior. The first time Rae had seen him, she had thought how at odds the expertly tailored suit and neatly knotted silk tie was with the man wearing it, so imposing and commanding was his physical presence. 'To say goodbye to Elena and tell *you* how sorry I am for your loss.'

The truth was she was more than sorry. That was too generic. She *ached* for him, physically and emotionally. That was why she had returned to Venice.

When she had read the news of Elena's passing, her first thought had been of Domenico. Her second had been of how to get to him in his time of suffering. Even now that she was here, closer than she had been to him in almost four months, it didn't feel close enough. The ten feet between them felt like ten thousand miles and something in her—the same instinct that had compelled her to return to Venice and Palazzo Ricci without a single beat of hesitation—longed to cross the space dividing them and wrap him in her arms.

And that was enough to trigger alarm bells in every corner of her body, because in dropping everything and racing to Domenico's side, hadn't she repeated her past mistakes? Fallen back into the dynamic that had made her so unhappy? And yes, it was an exceptional moment that she was probably right to make an exception for, but it was making her question whether she'd changed as much as she'd thought she had in the past months. And that was a very disquieting thought.

'Well, you've offered your condolences now,' he said, his eyes scraping over her in a merciless perusal which, despite their stoniness, roused tingles all over her skin. 'You're free to leave this home that pushed you into such misery. I would offer to walk you to the door, but I'm sure you remember where it is from the last time you walked out of it.'

With another scathing glower, he returned to his contemplation of the world outside the window.

A stinging heat crept into Rae's eyes and cheeks. She'd always known Domenico could be ruthless and cutting. Managing a global conglomerate with thousands of employees required it of him at times. But he did not like to have to be so, she knew that too, and she had certainly never been on the receiving end of his cold dismissal.

It was an indication of just how unhappy he was with her, how deep his anger ran. She had left him, scorned and humiliated him. He'd probably never wanted to set eyes on her again—wasn't that why he'd made no effort to chase after her?

Yet here she was.

Rae's heart rattled with uncertainty. Maybe she should do as he bade and leave. Domenico clearly didn't want her here. And she didn't *need* to be here. Estranged wives didn't have any particular role to play in family events, after all. He had the palazzo staff to take care of any practical needs and no doubt he had...*other companions* to cater to his emotional needs.

Thinking about it now, there had really been no reason at all for her to make the journey to Venice. It had been utterly stupid of her to come!

Rae had taken a few steps in retreat when she stopped, her mind suddenly abuzz with the unpleasant awareness that she was once again being cowed by Domenico's mood, and was reacting in the same way as she always had before—letting it shut her down. *Well, not this time*, she thought, remembering the promise she'd made to never let herself be silenced again.

She had returned to Venice because she was worried about him. Worried that Elena's passing would be a tragedy so big to contend with he wouldn't know where to start. Worried that no matter how many willing companions he had, he would not express the depth of his feelings. From personal experience, Rae knew that getting Domenico to open up was like trying to pry tectonic plates apart and nothing she had seen so far had convinced her that her fears were unfounded. So she would not do as he commanded and leave, not until she had done what she'd come to do, and so with a quiet sigh, steeling herself to face more of Domenico's wrath, she turned back, her steps drawing her closer to him.

'You want me leave and I will, okay. But first I want to make sure that you're doing as well as you can be right now. That's why I came,' Rae admitted, 'not just to offer my condolences. But to check on you.'

He released a bark of derision that seemed to convey a lot more than a single sound should. It seemed to question why, if she cared so much about his well-being, had she left him? And it was a fair question, she supposed. But her feelings for him had never been the issue, had they?

'I'm fine.'

Rae swallowed the urge to scream as he delivered his standard dismissive rebuff. Why did he always have to be so stubborn, so unwilling to lower his guard, even just an inch?

'Are you, Domenico? Really? How many of those have you had this afternoon?' she demanded, striding into his side vision and gesturing to the antique crystal tumbler cradled between his long-fingered hands. 'Have you eaten at all? Have you slept?'

'My sleeping arrangements are no longer any of your business, Rae.' He threw the words at her in a way that implied it was not his sleeping pattern to which he was referring but his sleeping partners and it left the mark it intended, lodging beneath her skin like a burning bullet.

'No, they're not,' she muttered, unable to fend off the image of him with another woman and instead fighting the surge of nausea that accompanied it. 'But I know the weight that grief places on a body, on a heart and a head. I know how the day feels endless, how all you crave is the oblivion of night and sleep, but when you get there, sleep won't come. I know how hard it is to do the ordinary things, like eat and move.' Having inclined his head, Domenico stared at her as though she were a witch, knowing things she shouldn't, that he would never willingly share. 'I've lived it too. Twice. Or had you forgotten that?'

Losing both of her parents in such a short space of time had been the hardest thing Rae had ever gone through. Most days she didn't know how she had survived that turmoil and emerged on the other side of it. She didn't credit herself as a particularly strong person—a person of any particular specialness, really—and she certainly didn't feel very strong in that moment, when being back in Domenico's orbit and subject to that astonishing force of his was only threatening to draw her back in. Making all the reasons why she'd had to leave feel so very minuscule, so very far away.

Making the warning bells jangle all over again.

'No.' Draining what was left in his glass, Domenico set it down and in the dim light of the nearby lamp she could see how ravaged he was by the events of the past days. In the lines bracketing his mouth and the shadows hugging his eyes, she could see his fatigue, his strain. His heartbreak. Never before had she seen such raw, naked emotion etched into his too handsome face and once more all she wanted to do was go to him and make it better, if only for a moment. 'I haven't forgotten. The death of a loved one is a wretched thing.' Something shifted behind his hard gaze as he turned the rest of his body to face her, leaning his hip against the large desk. 'I assumed that since you knew that sting of loss, you would value your relationships all the more. But how wrong I was.' His features shifted again, rearranging themselves into an expression that wasn't difficult to translate. 'You are a million miles away from the person I believed you to be.'

'Then I guess we both suffered the sting of that particular disappointment.' He'd not turned out to be the man she'd believed him to be either!

Outrage filled his face and fuelled a heavy breath. 'What disappointment did you ever have cause to feel? I gave you everything. I offered you everything.'

Rae could not and would never dispute that. Domenico had been unfailingly generous, at least materially, but it was the price of what he had given and offered that had been fatal to their relationship.

Be at his side always. Surrender all aspects of her own life. Place him and his needs ahead of her own, every single minute of every single day.

Doing so hadn't been hard. Considering him, wanting to do whatever she could to make his life a little easier when he shouldered such huge responsibilities without complaint had been easy. Making him happy had made her happy and what had made Domenico happy was having her beside him all the time. But then one day Rae had realised she had nothing of her own. No work. No friends. No hobbies. *No life.* Nothing to sustain her should she ever find herself alone again.

It was her worst nightmare come true.

Because she knew how that scenario ended. In desolation and depression.

She had watched it happen up close. She had lived it, powerless to do anything to stop the insidious spread of pain, though she had tried everything.

The thought of returning to that emotionally empty and destructive place terrified her, and with a husband who'd been entirely unwilling to help her make the space to build that fuller life she'd craved, Rae had feared it was a very real possibility.

Her stomach knotted with the strength of the remembered feeling, but Rae chased the discomfort away. The intention behind her return had not been to sift through the ashes of their marriage and she certainly wasn't going to do so on the day of Elena's burial and with a house full of mourners to overhear.

'I think we'll have to agree to disagree on that point,' Rae muttered tautly.

Domenico said nothing, and skewered her with a look that was part exasperation and part loathing. But there was something else lurking in the shadows too, something that added a flicker of excitement to her pulse, that same undefined thing she could feel humming just beneath her own skin—something too dangerous to be acknowledged for any longer than a nanosecond.

Taking a step back from it, and from him, Rae released the breath that she hadn't realised had been building in her chest. 'Downstairs is still full of guests, you know. You should be down there with them instead of up here alone.'

Her words were met with a stubborn silence, but then he exhaled a long breath. 'I'd rather be up here,' he said flatly. 'All anyone wants to tell me is how wonderful Elena was and I'm too furious with her right now to want to ruminate on her excellence.'

'Domenico…' Rae breathed, the admission making her heart ache for him.

His relationship with Elena had been a treasured part of his life and the moment Rae had met the older woman she had instantly seen why. Elena had had a formidable mind, a generous heart and beautiful spirit. She had also been the constant in Domenico's life and his only family, raising him from when he was a few days old and his biological mother, a young relation of Elena's, couldn't. Or wouldn't. Rae wasn't too sure. Whenever she had tried to dig deeper into Domenico's family history, she had been firmly and unmistakably rebuffed.

In fact, whenever Rae had tried to engage him in any conversation about his emotions or his life, Domenico had shut her down. From the moment they'd met she'd sensed he was burdened by whatever had occurred in the past, but whilst he'd been happy to let her close physically, to even use their sexual chemistry as a way of silencing her questions, emotionally he had never let her in, always holding her at arm's length.

At one point in time Rae had thought their respective trauma would be something to bind them even closer together. Something they could share with each other that they couldn't with others. She had never imagined it would break them apart instead. But of all the matters that Domenico had refused to open himself up about, his unwillingness to trust her with any of the details about his family situation had cut deep. Because how could she live with someone who didn't want her to know him? How could she keep giving up so much of her own life and self for a man who wouldn't show her his heart?

However, in that moment his hurt was all too easy to see and, feeling that pain, Rae could no longer keep herself from moving towards him. It was the most natural thing to want to go to him, to slide her hands up his arms, across his shoulders and wind them around his neck and hold him tight. Let him know that he wasn't alone. Domenico was a physical being and physical touch had always been the best way to reach him, to breach the weight and distraction of a long day or stressful negotiation. To encourage him to open up. And Rae couldn't bear the thought of him isolating himself in his grief, in his understandable anger.

She remembered being furious in the aftermath of her father's death. How was it fair that it was him who had been taken too soon, her father and not anybody else's? Why did she and her sisters have to go on with their lives without their integral cog? She was certain Domenico would be feeling something similar. His spectacularly strong build made him look untouchable, but he had such capacity for feeling, experiencing every emotion sharply, deeply.

But she had only just reached out to him when the lift of his cold eyes halted her as if she'd been turned to stone.

'What are you doing?'

'I'm…'

'Is this why you came?' he demanded, his eyes still pools of darkness as they probed her face, as if the answers were writing themselves across her skin, when all she could feel was a tormented, scorching heat filling her cheeks. 'Were you hoping the opportunity would arise for you to comfort me and I'd fall back into your arms?' She was too stunned to speak. 'Even griefstricken I am not that stupid. You made it clear how little you care for me and that's not something I'll forget in a hurry, so I suggest you turn around and keep walking out of the door this time.'

He gestured towards the door with his hand, his eyes remaining fixed on her with a stoniness that turned her stomach inside out.

Rae had always known he'd be furious with her. Domenico, after all, was not used to others calling the shots. But with time she'd expected he would come to see that she had been right, that they wanted irreconcilable futures, and her leaving had been for the best. It had never crossed her mind that he'd *stay* so angry.

She hadn't wanted to hurt him. She'd just been trying to keep herself from becoming any more overwhelmed. Since talking to him had never yielded any positive results before, there'd been no reason to believe that he would *hear* her had she tried to do so again, so it had been easier to not try. To just leave. And nothing about his unwilling stance before her was making her think she'd been wrong to believe that.

But still, her throat was thick as she slowly turned towards the door and instructed her numbed legs to move.

'Actually, I think it might be a good idea for Rae to stay.'

The intrusion had both of their heads lifting sharply. Elena's lawyer and the Riccis' long-time family friend, Alessandra Donati, paused in the doorway, surveying them mildly.

'*Che cosa? Perché?*' Domenico demanded of her hotly, surveying her with his hands planted on his hips and a look that threatened to carve her in two.

Alessandra appeared unconcerned. 'I think Rae

should stay for the reading of the will tomorrow. She is, after all, family and I'm sure Elena would have wanted her here.'

Rae tried to hide her surprise that Alessandra, of all people, was speaking in her defence. Having known her since arriving in Venice, she had never been given any indication that she could consider her any type of ally.

Unleashing a curse in fervent Italian, Domenico seemed to struggle with controlling his body. 'Are you seriously telling me that my aunt included her in her will?' A look of incredulity had cut itself into the beautiful planes of his face.

'I'm not telling you anything,' Alessandra parried calmly. 'Elena's final wishes will be revealed tomorrow, for everyone to hear at the same time. But my advice to both of you is that now that Rae is here, she should stay.'

Alessandra matched Domenico's hard gaze, some kind of exchange passing between them, and Rae felt a pinch of jealousy that there seemed to be no problem with *their* communication.

Overcoming his perplexed bewilderment, Domenico looked from Alessandra to Rae and then back again, his emotion building by the second if the shade of his face was anything to judge by. *'Bene.'* He threw up his hands. 'Fine. She will stay.'

'I don't...' Rae began, before falling silent beneath the quelling look Domenico dealt her. She looked instead to Alessandra. 'What time is the reading tomorrow?'

'Ten a.m. Here at the palazzo.'

She nodded her understanding, her throat tight with the thought of being such a patently unwanted guest at such a personal event. But she could hardly challenge it now, even if that was what she desperately wanted to do. 'I will see you both tomorrow then.'

Alessandra smiled at her and slipped away and Rae decided it was past time she did the same. The encounter with Domenico had left her feeling off-balance and drained and in need of a long shower and then a soft bed.

'Where do you think you are going?' Domenico queried as she took her first steps towards the door.

'Back to my hotel.'

'I don't think so. You'll stay here.'

Rae's heart slammed into her ribs at the thought of remaining in the palazzo, where memoires lurked around every corner, memories that were so incredibly potent. Walking through the front doors earlier and remembering how Domenico had once carried her through them had blocked her throat and brought her close to tears. As she'd climbed the staircase, with each step she had recalled all the times Domenico had led her up them, her hand in his, promise in his eyes whenever he'd looked back at her.

'That's not necessary. I have a…'

Domenico's face darkened. 'Don't test me, Rae. Not today. I don't trust you one bit. So you will stay here, where I can keep an eye on you.'

'Keep an eye on me?' She couldn't keep the disbelief from her voice, not when he made her sound like a wayward charge. 'What is it that you imagine I am going to do?'

'I won't pretend to know your mind,' he hit back, and it was another heavyweight blow straight to her middle because he was the first person that Rae had allowed to know her in her adult life. She realised now that he hadn't known all of her, not the parts of herself that she'd lost or concealed in her effort to be the wife she'd thought he'd wanted, but he remained the first, and only, person she had let close to her after the horror of losing her parents. 'But until I know exactly what involvement you have in Elena's will, I want you where I can see you. I will have Portia show you where you can sleep tonight.'

It was unsurprising to her that Domenico wrested complete control as usual, blatantly ignoring her wishes and her needs. No, not ignoring—not even asking!

Rae bristled with a fury that had her opening her mouth to vent the protest already on her tongue, but she was suddenly too exhausted to argue. Instead, she nodded and let herself be led away by Portia when she arrived, content to let Domenico have his way in that moment because once she'd benefitted from a restoring full night's sleep, and felt more like herself, she had no intention of letting it happen again.

She had changed, and the days of her silently acquiescing to his decisions and wishes were well and truly over.

CHAPTER TWO

DOMENICO PROWLED AROUND the gilded darkness of the palazzo like a restless animal. There was too much emotion coursing through his body for him to rest easily, either asleep or awake. The hours he had just spent in his private gym, pushing himself on the treadmill and punching until his knuckles felt raw, had succeeded in exhausting his muscles but had failed to rid him of his aggravating emotions.

Damn Rae.

Damn her for leaving and damn her for coming back.

He had far too many other matters in need of careful handling to be giving any thought to the wife who had walked out on him, and yet from the moment he had turned away from the window and settled his hard eyes on her, his only thoughts had been of her body. Wrapped around him. Welcoming him inside her.

He had very much wanted to sweep her onto his desk, part her legs, slip into the warm space between her thighs and bury himself inside her. He craved the velvet welcome her body had always offered, her muscles contracting and then clenching around him, her sweet heat enveloping him, urging him to sink deeper.

He had been shaking with the force of the wanting, and the effort required to resist it.

Because he refused to want her. After the way she had abandoned him, desiring her was not an option.

But there had never been anything tame or cooperative about his feelings for Rae. The first time he'd seen her, standing outside Venice's airport, looking unbelievably attractive in an all-black ensemble, the natural highlights in her chestnut hair glinting in the low sun, he had wanted her immediately. Wanted to know who she was and to have her in his bed. Beneath him. On top of him. And in the hundred other ways flying through his mind. The potency of the desire had stopped him in his tracks on the busy pavement, bludgeoning all other thoughts from his mind, and the charge that had rocked his big body had been so electrifying it was as though he'd been struck by a bolt of lightning.

That fevered desire for her hadn't abated as he had expected it to, as had been usual in his previous relationships—if they could really be called that. Far from satisfying the craving, claiming her body as his own had only intensified his hunger for her and very quickly that scorching want had morphed into a *need* that he hadn't seen coming.

A need to keep her close. A need for her smile and her piercing blue eyes to be the first thing he saw when he opened his eyes each morning. A need to have the warmth of her body beside his all day, every day.

None of his past relationships had triggered anything so domestic in him, but none of those women had given him what Rae had seemed to be giving—her wholehearted acceptance and warmth and love. Oh, she hadn't said the words, but Domenico had known she was falling in love with him. Knew it by the way her eyes tracked his movements, by the way she took every opportunity to touch him—light brushes of her hand, tender grazes of her lips—and by the way she snuggled in close at night.

It had been addictive, so much so that Domenico had actually been unhappy about their affair ending when it was time for Rae to return home, but he hadn't expected that melancholy mood to last for more than a day, two at the most. To his surprise, however, he'd found himself missing her at all kinds of odd moments, missing her so much that eventually he'd given in and hopped on a jet to London. He'd surprised her when she finished work, waiting outside the bridal boutique where she was a consultant, and the smile that had lit her face when she'd spotted him had been dazzling. He couldn't remember a time when someone other than Elena had been that happy to see him, and as she'd thrown herself into his arms Domenico had felt something tight and knotted within him loosen, certain in that moment that life would be better if Rae was always by his side. Lowering her to the ground, he'd gazed down at her and said, *'Marry me...'* the words bubbling up inside him.

Her response had been instantaneous. *'Yes.'*

Four weeks later they had been married in Venice. Domenico had refused to wait any longer than that, wanting the marriage to be official as quickly as possible, wanting their claim on each other to be inviolable, wanting that new chapter of his life with a wife who loved him and would always be at his side to begin.

As the recollections crashed through his mind, Domenico cursed under his breath, hating the memories and their power. Hating his own stupidity. Had he really believed that Rae had loved him above all else and in a way that no one had loved him before? It seemed laughable now and he was riddled with detestation for his own pathetic weakness. For allowing himself to be so caught up in how good it felt to be wanted by someone, to be claimed by them for all to witness. After being rejected by his mother and never formally adopted by Elena, marriage to Rae had given him something that he'd never had before—acceptance and validation. Belonging.

But to be given something and then have it ripped away…that was crueller than never knowing it in the first place, and that was exactly what Rae had done.

Never again would he put himself at the mercy of another human being. Never again would he trust. The only silver lining to Rae's betrayal was that it had awoken him to his own weaknesses and in many ways that had been worth all the pain…

The pain of returning home, aching to see her face and feel her soft hands smooth over his tight shoulders, only to learn she was gone, that she had left him… stopped loving him…rejected him.

It was only as Domenico came to a sudden stop to pause the wayward trajectory of his thoughts and the leaden kicks of his heart that he took in his surroundings and realised that, whilst lost in his memories, he had paced up to Elena's suite of rooms on the second highest floor of the palazzo. In spite of his many pleas to her to relocate to a lower floor to make her movements less arduous, she had consistently refused, unwilling to give up her views of the city or the rooms that had been hers since she'd moved into the palazzo as a young bride. The memory made him ache deep in his chest and Domenico was on the verge of turning away, as it was still way too soon for him to be able to go near her personal space, when he noticed the door was ajar and a slice of light was spilling through the crack.

Eyes narrowed in query, he reached for the door, but suddenly it was pulled open from the other side and Rae emerged, her movements stilling and eyes flying wide when she saw him standing there.

Domenico suppressed a growl. Was there no escape from her? Was she determined to haunt him in his own house as well as his mind?

'I'm sorry,' she said, frozen in the doorway like a rabbit in the headlights. She was dressed in a short silk pyjama set, her hair contained in the same low ponytail she'd worn earlier. He had always preferred her hair down, loose and spilling over her shoulders for his fingers to run through, and from the early days of their relationship he'd liked her to come to bed in something he'd enjoy ripping off, and whilst this was definitely not that, he found himself growing hard as his eyes devoured every inch of her. 'I didn't mean to intrude. I just… I couldn't sleep and I was thinking about Elena and I wanted to feel close to her and say some kind of goodbye so I came up here…' She swallowed as she took in his unchanging expression. 'But that was clearly the wrong thing to do. I'm sorry. I'm leaving.'

Domenico's instinct was to send her scurrying away even faster with the rebuke that had she not left she wouldn't need to say a goodbye, but then he noticed the emotion sparkling in her eyes and the reproach melted on his tongue. He knew Rae had loved and respected Elena enormously and that in many ways his aunt had filled the void left by the loss of her parents. One of Rae's favourite things had been exploring Elena's cavernous closet, studying her one-of-a-kind gowns, and Elena had delighted in regaling her with the story of each one. Her sudden death had to be stirring up difficult memories for Rae.

'It's fine. You're entitled to say goodbye to her. I know how much you cared for her and Elena was incredibly fond of you too. Don't rush away on my account,' he said with a sigh that was wrenched from him, because the sudden tenderness of feeling was so unwanted.

'Thank you.' Her mouth opened, only for her to hesitate before deciding to press on. 'Did Elena… I'm not aware of how she passed away…and I was just wondering if she suffered.'

'The pathologist said it was most likely an aneurism. That it would have been fast, almost instantaneous. Painless. She probably wouldn't have known.'

'Good. I'm glad. I'd hate to think that she'd been in any pain.'

Her gaze shimmered again and something erupted in Domenico's chest, a feeling of such power it felt as if his lungs were being squeezed by giant hands. He'd always hated to see Rae upset, the sight slicing right to the heart of him, and acting on the instinct firing up from a place deep within him, he reached out, curling his hand to her cheek and tenderly wiping away the tears with his thumb.

A shudder ran across his chest as the feel of the warm silk of her skin had an even bolder surge of desire pumping through his veins, forcing him to remember just how long it had been since he had satisfied his carnal cravings, since he had lost himself in the tight heat of a woman's body. If there was ever a time he could do with drowning himself in someone else, this was it. And he had never generated a more compelling heat than the one he did with Rae...

Instinct flared again, more primal than before, and Domenico lowered his thumb, tracing it across her pillow-soft lower lip, and the pure blue of her eyes exploded with a hunger that set them aflame.

With such potent desire hammering within him and forcing everything else from his mind, including all his reasons for loathing her, all Domenico could feel was his impatient pounding *want*. Raising his other hand, he captured her face between his palms and with one, two, three easy steps he had her backed against the nearest wall. Her dazed eyes held his as he stared hungrily down at her, his heart and pulse pounding in perfect synchronisation as his gaze traced the shape of her face—her flushed cheeks, her delicate jaw, her parted lips.

'Domenico...'

Was that a warning or a plea? He didn't know, or care, because his name on her tongue, in her whispered breath, nearly undid him. All he needed to do was press in a centimetre closer, lower his mouth, and he could ease the agitated ache beating in his blood and taste her on his lips again—a taste he had been craving ever since she'd left.

He froze, that final thought echoing around his brain. She had left him.

So what the hell was he doing?

With a quiet growl of frustration, he pulled himself back, putting distance between their bodies and trying to smother his heavy breaths. 'It's late. You should go back to your room, get some sleep. You've had a long day,' he instructed, sounding far more in control than he felt.

Rae blinked slowly, the daze slowly draining from her gaze. 'Yes, you're right. I should do that.' Slowly, almost unsteadily, she peeled herself off the wall, colour still flaming in her cheeks. She moved gingerly towards the staircase. 'Goodnight.'

'Buona notte,' he rasped, raking a hand through his hair and willing the beating of his blood to subside.

When it didn't, he marched back to his suite and straight into the shower, setting the temperature as cold as it would go, cold enough to kill entirely the traitorous desire that continued to burn in his blood.

The reading of Elena's will would take place in one of the large salons on the ground floor of the palazzo. It was not customary to have such a formal reading where Rae hailed from—they'd read her father's will around the kitchen table—but there was nothing regular about the Ricci family. Wealth and status like theirs, she'd long ago learned, demanded grander formalities. So, at five minutes to ten, Rae unsteadily descended the staircase, armed with her plan to slip in unnoticed, take a seat near the door and leave as soon as the proceedings were over. Her small case was already packed and waiting by the main door, so she didn't have to spend any longer in the palazzo than was necessary.

Her hopes were dashed almost immediately. The moment Rae entered the grand room, Alessandra excused herself from the conversation she was in and made straight for her, greeting her with a friendly smile and a kiss to each cheek.

'I have a seat for you,' she announced.

'Oh, I was just going to find somewhere here at the back…' Rae began, motioning to the very last row of seats, but Alessandra was shaking her head.

'Absolutely not. You're family, Rae. And family sits at the front.'

'I'm not sure Domenico will like that,' she replied tightly.

'This isn't about him. It's about Elena,' Alessandra parried, gesturing for Rae to follow her to the front of the salon and indicating a chair on the front row, right next to the seat occupied by the broad shoulders and proud back of Domenico. He was dressed in another black suit, neat and exquisitely fitted to his broad form, and he looked exceptional, far more so than anyone in a state of grief should.

'Are you going to sit on the chair or just continue to stare at it?' Domenico posed with a dark arch of his brow and, with a resigned sigh, Rae sat. But, as she did, her arm brushed against his and heat crackled through her, making her instantly feverish as remembrance of the previous night crashed through her.

She had spent the better part of the night wide awake and trying not to think about what had exploded between them. How he had framed her face in his strong hands, how she'd been trapped between the wall and his very solid, very hot body, how his lips had been right *there*, a mere breath from hers. The fact that nothing had actually happened didn't ease the alarm she felt, because something very easily *could* have happened. It had been on the cusp of happening. She had been seconds away from begging for his mouth to be on her— her lips, her breasts, her… *No!*

Rae knew her only hope now was to leave as soon as possible. If she got away quickly, she could consign the previous night's events to some dusty shelf in the far recesses of her mind and, within a matter of weeks, hopefully it would be as if it had never happened. As if none of the emotional upheaval of her ill-thought-out trip had happened.

'You slept well, I hope,' Domenico said suddenly, without tuning his head to look at her.

'The room was very comfortable,' Rae answered noncommittally, because there was no way she wanted him to have a single idea of how unsettled he'd left her.

'You didn't sleep?' he pressed, and this time he did turn his head and she was swallowed up by his bottomless dark gaze. His regard was as hot and heavy as his physical touch had been and Rae's mouth ran dry, her lips tingled and a pulse ignited between her legs.

She squeezed her thighs together, but it failed to quash the reaction pounding through her. The liquid heat of need raced through her veins, making her hunger for his touch all over again, and suddenly all she could feel was the sensation of falling. That she was tumbling head over heels into him and wanting nothing more than to be back in that hallway last night, caged by his delectable male body.

From what sounded like far away Rae heard a female voice—Alessandra—calling everyone to attention and asking them to take their seats—and she clung to it, using it as a lifeline to grip onto as she tried to drag herself from her sensual freefall.

'I slept fine, thank you,' she said, cleaving her gaze from Domenico's and fixing her attention straight ahead. She forced herself to ignore the sirens wailing in her body and listen to every single one of Alessandra's welcoming and introductory words before she handed over the duties to the other executor of Elena's estate, Elena's long-time friend and confidant, Vincenzo D'Aragona. Very quickly, his smooth baritone voice filled the salon.

One more hour, Rae estimated as Vincenzo began on the bequests, and then she would be on her way home. The thought brought a little bit of calm to her galloping heart because she wasn't sure how many more moments like that with Domenico she could withstand.

Exhaling shakily, Rae tuned back in to the reading of the will. Vincenzo was in the middle of stating Elena's wish that her donations to certain charities continued from her estate. Then he moved on to the individual bequests, monetary gifts and heirlooms for specific friends and family—none of which surprised Rae, as Elena had always been extraordinarily generous.

'Finally, to the matters of business and real estate. It was Elena's wish that all of her shares in The Ricci Group pass in totality to her named heir, Domenico Paolo Ricci. Her real estate portfolio, including but not limited to her homes in Rome and Lake Como and the apartment in Paris, will also pass to Domenico Paolo Ricci. However,' Vincenzo continued with a pregnant pause, during which Alessandra cast something of an uneasy glance Domenico's way and, noticing it, a slither of unease stirred in Rae's stomach, 'with regard to Palazzo Ricci here in Venice, Elena insisted upon the addition of a marital clause and in the event that Domenico fails to meet the stated requirements of said clause, Palazzo Ricci will pass to Elena's next closest living relative, her sister.'

The gasps of surprise from others were quickly quelled with a stern look from Vincenzo. Face tight but expressionless, Domenico leaned slightly forward, biceps straining against the confines of the suit.

'In this case, the marital clause stipulates that Domenico will only inherit on the celebration of the second anniversary of his wedding to his wife Raegan Dunbar-Ricci on October the second this year.'

Domenico went rigid, but it was an extra second before it hit Rae. And, once it did, her eyes flew wide.

What?

CHAPTER THREE

DOMENICO PACED back and forth over the same length of
floor. If he thought about it hard enough, he knew he
would find a way out of the situation, some clever escape hatch…but each turn of his thoughts only brought
him back to the same place, the same damnable words
of Elena's will clanging over and over again in his mind.

'Are you okay?'

Having thought he was alone, Domenico quickly
drew to a stop and raised his head. Alessandra stood
in front of the closed door and Domenico pinioned her
under his furious glare.

'What do you think?' Solely by virtue of the self-
control honed meticulously over the years, he had managed to regulate his reaction for the remainder of the
reading and the interminable process of bidding everyone goodbye, but the tether around his frustration
was now frayed perilously thin. 'I can't believe you
knew this was going to happen and didn't warn me,'
he hissed, the sting of her treachery arrowing deeper
into his skin.

At least now, however, he understood why Alessandra had been so insistent that Rae stay and attend the

will reading—but he was far too angry to feel any gratitude to her.

'You know very well the contents of a will have to remain private until after a person's death,' Alessandra reproached him. 'I was doing my job, Domenico. It's nothing personal.'

'It's personal to me,' he snarled.

'And is that all that is angering you?' Alessandra queried levelly.

'Isn't that enough?'

'So it's not about Rae's involvement in Elena's stipulation?' She allowed her words to hang in mid-air for a second before continuing. 'I won't pretend to know what's going on in your marriage, Domenico, but there's obviously something. Rae has been gone for weeks and you've been in a less than pleasant mood for most of that time.'

He spun away to stare moodily out of the window, fixing his arms across his chest. 'The state of my marriage is nobody's business but mine and Rae's.'

But as he bit out the words, Domenico knew that wasn't the case any more. A spotlight had been placed on their union—the union on which something incredibly precious to him now rested.

With superhuman effort, he swallowed the curse surging up his throat. Elena had orchestrated it perfectly, forcing his hand from beyond the grave with her stipulation. She knew Domenico would never willingly relinquish ownership of the palazzo, the only home he'd ever known, especially not to the blood relatives who had denied and rejected him, and the last thing she'd want either was her beloved palazzo ending up in the hands of her estranged sister. For both of those reasons she'd known full well he would do *anything* to prevent that from happening, including reuniting with Rae.

Which was exactly what his aunt had wanted. How many times had she prodded him to go to London, talk to Rae and fix whatever had broken down between them? So often that he'd lost count, but, since he'd flatly refused to do so, she'd decided to take matters into her own hands.

Devious and manipulative as it was, he found he couldn't be angry with her. Even in death, Elena was still trying to protect and take care of him in the same way she always had and, eternal romantic that she was, she'd believed Rae was *the one* for him. No doubt she'd thought that she could prompt a permanent reunion by forcing them back together for an extended period of time.

But, however much Domenico hated to disappoint Elena, that wasn't going to happen.

Rae had walked out on him without a backward glance. She had shown herself to be as careless and unfeeling as the mother who'd abandoned him on someone else's doorstep. There would be no second chance.

He would never open himself up to more anguish. If there was any other option other than reconciling with Rae, he would take it. But he knew that nothing other than him and Rae being visibly happy together in his palazzo in Venice would satisfy the esteemed Vincenzo D'Aragona, the man Elena had named as executor of her will and therefore the man who would make the final decision on whether Domenico's circumstances complied with the will. He was a thoroughly unimpeachable character who had counselled Elena ever since her husband's death, with unfailing loyalty and affection. Domenico had no doubt that he would follow her wishes absolutely.

Even if D'Aragona had been a less noble character, Domenico was astute enough to know that anything less than the appearance of wedded bliss would leave him vulnerable to a future legal challenge and he wouldn't risk the palazzo in that way. It meant too much to him.

His conviction on that was stronger than anything he felt about Rae or the wretched will.

Closing his eyes and rubbing his temples, he faced the irrefutable facts of the situation and plotted his next step. There was only one.

'Where are you going?' Alessandra asked as he made a sudden and decisive move towards the door without a word to her.

'To talk to my wife.'

He really should have spoken with Rae immediately after the reading had ended, because he'd known all along there was only one way out of this mess. But he had needed a moment—several moments—to himself to process it, something he bitterly began to regret as he arrived on the ground floor salon and scanned all four corners, only to find that the room was empty.

With dread starting to roil in his stomach and that loud voice in his head berating him for leaving her alone, Domenico set his powerful legs in motion and raced into the next room and then the next, but in his gut he already knew the search was pointless.

Rae was already gone.

Rae pushed her sunglasses atop her head to keep her long hair from flying in her face as the water taxi raced across the open water to Marco Polo Airport. Yet as she imagined the violent reaction Domenico would have when he realised she had slipped away without a word—*again*—the speed felt nowhere near enough and she willed the boat to go faster.

Casting a quick look over her shoulder, the reassurance she felt that there was no sign of a vessel powering after her was hollow as she knew that by now Domenico had probably realised she had taken off and would be minutes away from—if not already—hunting her down.

Rae felt awful for sneaking away, but really, what other choice had there been? Elena's bombshell stipulation in her will had changed everything, and now that Domenico's inheritance of the palazzo was contingent on their union—on *her*—she had known at once there was no way he was going to let her leave.

And she couldn't stay. She couldn't!

She had been back in Venice less than twenty-four hours and there had been too many moments in which she'd caught herself falling back into her old ways. And not just physically, as the previous night attested, when Domenico's touch had penetrated her with embarrassing speed and ease. But emotionally too. For a brief moment back at the palazzo, after the will reading, Rae had been preoccupied with all that it meant for Domenico, reflecting on what *he* must be feeling and what *he* needed, prioritising that over what was best for herself. In the blink of an eye, she'd reverted to the Rae of six months ago, to the wife who never spoke up for herself, who hadn't been brave enough to demand that her needs be met, who hadn't known herself well enough to even know what those needs were.

But she wasn't that person any more. The issues that had arisen in their marriage had been enlightening, forcing her to take a good look inwards and consider the life she wanted to have and the kind of woman she wanted to be and, unwilling to let all the agony and heartache of the breakdown of her marriage be for nothing, Rae had wasted no time in fighting to become that person on her return to London.

Reconnecting with her ambition to become a bridal designer, Rae had dusted off her pencils and thrown herself back into the creative process of designing. No longer willing to wait for life to happen to her, she had even screwed up enough courage to contact the woman who'd once offered to invest in her should she ever decide to embark on a career in bridal design and, after her positive response, had been busy making plans for a full-blown collection. Immersing herself in her passion and with her eyes fixed on the bright future that she wanted for herself, Rae had regained her confidence and her voice.

It had never been her intention to surrender those aspects of herself, to lose herself so thoroughly in being with Domenico and the responsibilities she bore as a Ricci bride. But she'd loved him so deeply and wanted so badly to make him happy that, little by little, all else had slipped away.

When she'd become aware of how adrift she'd been feeling, she'd wanted to tell Domenico, to find a way to change. But he'd always been so closed off, always ready to retreat from any intimacy that wasn't physical, and Rae had been scared of being shut down yet again, scared of having to face how tenuous their relationship was. Running had been easier than challenging him, easier than confronting the hard truths about their marriage, but in her heart Rae knew she should have tried harder to have that conversation. A lot harder.

It was a regret that surfaced often, and whenever that thought did poke at her she comforted herself with the reassurance that she had changed and would not lack that courage or conviction again.

But she had, she realised with a nauseating thud of her heart.

Rather than stay at the palazzo and talk with Domenico about their situation, she had panicked and run away. *Again.*

The water taxi drew up to the airport. Rae thrust a handful of euros into the driver's hand and stepped up onto dry land, that sick feeling continuing to churn in her stomach as she pulled up the handle of her case and strode across the concrete concourse. Only to suddenly find she could take no further steps.

Because if she left like this she knew it would be another regret that haunted her. Not just because she would be condemning Domenico to the loss of his treasured home, but because running away wasn't the answer. It hadn't been last time and it wasn't now either. If she truly believed she had changed, and wanted others to appreciate those changes in her too, then she needed to prove herself. Prove that she was different, that she was stronger. That she wasn't a coward.

Sinking down onto a bench to allow time for her thoughts to settle, it was there that Domenico found her not fifteen minutes later. Standing before her, he towered over her, casting her in the shade of his big body that even in that moment had her breath catching in her chest.

'I expected you to be on the first flight out of here by now,' he said, his eyes flickering over her as though unsure if she was real.

'That was the original plan.'

'So what happened?'

'I realised that running away wouldn't solve anything. We have to face this.'

She saw something—surprise, perhaps—ripple through his dark eyes before he sat down beside her, her body jolting a little at the sudden nearness and the way the air seemed to change, thicken, with his presence.

'I'm glad you understand what needs to happen next.'

Rae angled her face towards him, injecting a look of warning into her eyes. 'I haven't agreed to anything, Domenico.'

'Of course you have,' he drawled all-knowingly. 'Otherwise, you wouldn't be sitting out here. You would be sitting on a plane, waiting to take off.' He looked at her almost sympathetically. 'It's only for a handful of months, Rae. Six at the most. Not an enormous amount of time in the grand scheme of things.'

He was right. Six months was not such a long stretch, but her heart gave a kick anyway because it was a struggle to spend six minutes in his proximity without a fever stirring in her blood.

'Aren't you at all concerned that we haven't been together for the last four months?' she queried, because that was a pertinent fact that he seemed to be conveniently ignoring. 'That I have not been in this city, or your home, or on your arm for all that time? Do you not think that's going to present a few problems? One day I'm not here and then *boom*, Elena's will stipulates it and suddenly I'm back.'

'Elena's will is not common knowledge. It's a private family document.'

Rae made a noise of dissent. 'You and I both know these things have a way of getting out. Making the rounds as a rumour.'

'I've never much cared for rumours,' he drawled, his eyes gleaming down at her in a way that made her head spin and all coherent thoughts scatter like marbles. 'And your argument will not be a problem as nobody is aware that you walked out on our marriage.'

'Nobody is aware…' Rae stammered in stunned disbelief, her mind doing backflips at the preposterousness of his statement. 'How is that possible? I left. I haven't been here for months. I haven't been seen. Nobody questioned that?'

'I'm not in the habit of making public declarations about my personal life,' he stated in that cool, unconcerned tone of his that stymied so effectively the questions he didn't want to answer. 'And something about my general demeanour seems to prevent the majority of people from probing too deeply. Those who did ask, I made a vague reply about you having a family situation that required your personal attention and attendance. We can continue with that line, say the issue is no longer pressing and, given the situation here, it was time for you to return home.'

'And which of my sisters do you intend to saddle with some mysterious prolonged drama that required my attention for four months?' she demanded. 'Maggie or Imogen?'

Domenico replied with a pragmatic lift of his shoulders. 'The particulars are hardly necessary. The less said, the better. All that matters is that you are back with your husband and living a happy life.'

The panic that had settled once she took control of herself started a slow climb up her windpipe again.

'Domenico, we are not just going to pick up where we left off, like nothing has happened. We can't... I won't,' Rae stammered.

'Nor would I want to. I'm not talking about us resuming our married life, Rae,' he clarified with a sharp edge of impatience to his words. 'The idea of that is as offensive to me as it apparently is to you. I'm talking about *pretending*. Putting on a blissfully happy show—a show good enough to convince Vincenzo D'Aragona. I'm confident the pretence won't be too arduous for you. After all, you did spend considerably longer than six months pretending to be a devoted, happy wife.'

'And just how many remarks like that would I be expected to put up with in our joyous reunion?' Rae queried with a lightning flash of her blue eyes.

'The truth is painful, Rae, isn't it? But worry not, our contact over the next six months will be limited. Of course, in public we'll need to present a deliriously in love front, and we'll need to attend a fair number of public events, but in private we won't need to spend any time together at all.'

'Why six months? Our anniversary is in four and a half.'

He slanted her a brief look. 'We can't suddenly split up the day after our anniversary, Rae. Think how that would look. No, we need a buffer period too, so that when we do separate it looks real. Plus the Ricci Ball is a month after our anniversary. It would look better if we attended that together. Some time after that we can start to dissolve the marriage. Leak some rumours of fighting and unhappiness. The strain of Elena's passing, the stress of stepping into her shoes. How busy I am. There are plenty of things we could say. Then we'll divorce. I'll have the palazzo and you can…go your own way.'

'You have it all worked out, don't you?' she breathed, conceding to herself that it did sound plausible.

He tensed, impatience and determination emanating from him in one jagged pulse after another. 'I'm not prepared to lose the palazzo, Rae. It's means too much to me. So I will do whatever it takes. But I can't do it on my own. I need your help. I need you to stay here. *Please.*'

His use of that word was startling in itself, because Domenico never pleaded for anything. He would consider it an abhorrence to do so, a lowering of himself that he simply wouldn't entertain, even in thought. It revealed how desperately in need he was of her cooperation, a desperation that became even clearer when he turned the power of his gaze on her and the restless emotion brimming in the dark depths of his eyes tugged at every heartstring.

'As soon as the inheritance is settled, we will go our separate ways and I will ensure you are rewarded with a generous sum.'

'I don't want your money, Domenico.' Rae scowled, loathing that his opinion of her had sunk so low that his instinctive assumption was that she could be swayed by the promise of a payout. His money had never mattered to her.

She was, however, intrigued by the other opportunities that a return to Venice presented. The way she had departed had left matters unfinished between her and Domenico. She had shut him out of her mind as best she could, but she was not over him, no matter how much she insisted to her sisters that she was. Wasn't that why she had not yet taken the step of approaching a lawyer to initiate a divorce? But perhaps these six months could help her find that longed for closure. Perhaps being around him and not sacrificing or compromising anything of herself would reassure her that she had become a different person and that she had made the right choice in leaving. And when the six months was over she would be able to leave the right way, with her conscience and confidence intact and her emotional freedom reclaimed. Helping Domenico was the right thing to do, she didn't doubt that, but it was those ways in which she could help herself that convinced her.

'And you don't need to dangle any more incentives. I'll help you. I'll be your wife again.'

'Thank you.' The words were ground from between his firm lips, but Rae could hear the relief in them and that strength of feeling had her mind humming with curiosity about his past once more. Why did Palazzo Ricci mean so very much to him? How had it ended up becoming his home and Elena his guardian? What had happened to his parents? Why hadn't they kept him?

They were just a few of the questions niggling away at her brain, but Rae had so many more that she would have loved the answers to and maybe, she thought with a flicker of interest, the following months would give her the opportunity to find those answers. That would certainly be an added and worthwhile bonus, especially if it helped her put to rest her relationship with him.

Rae got to her feet, adopting a straight-backed pose as she quickly worked out the necessary practicalities. 'I'll go back to London, tie up some ends there and be back in a few days.'

Confusion pulled Domenico's dark brows together as he rose too. 'What do you mean, you will go back to London?' He shook his head. 'You can't leave, Rae.'

'I need to. For starters, these are the only clothes I have with me...' she began, gesturing to the garments adorning her body.

'There are plenty of shops here in Venice,' he cut in with impatience and frustration. 'And your wardrobe at the palazzo has not been touched.'

The thought of slipping back into the clothes of that past life left Rae cold. She had no desire or intention to go backwards and as such his implacable, inconsiderate interruption had her gritting her teeth and replying with forced patience. 'I have responsibilities in London. I'm not prepared to just abandon them.'

His brows pleated even tighter, his eyes darkening as her refusal to fall in line registered. He'd never known her to be anything other than amenable and accommodating to his wishes and the change was so disconcerting to him, he couldn't hide it.

But then his eyes narrowed. 'What responsibilities?' he questioned.

'A job. Bills. My sisters.'

Domenico continued to assess her, thoughts whizzing across his eyes like shooting stars and his jaw tightening in uneasy consideration. 'Is a man the source of this need to return to London so quickly?'

'What?' Rae very nearly laughed, so outrageous was the thought.

He moved in a step closer. 'You heard me.'

She shook her head, still fighting the urge to laugh, which was so at odds with the severity of his expression. 'No. There's no one.'

'Because I will not be made a fool of by you for the second time, and that is exactly the type of detail that would undermine my claim and make this whole charade for nothing. So, if that is the case, you need to tell me now,' he commanded with godlike presumption.

Provoked by both his words and his tone, Rae stepped up to him, tilting her head back so their eyes collided, hers fizzing with anger whilst his remained darkly unyielding.

'Firstly, I don't have to tell you anything I don't want to,' she began audaciously, 'in much the same way you never told me anything you didn't want to. But, on this occasion, I am prepared to tell you that there is no one. Secondly, this isn't a negotiation,' she said, her spine and her stance strengthening with her newly acquired confidence and conviction. 'I *am* going back to London. I'll be gone forty-eight hours, three days at the most. Then I'll be back and the masquerade can begin.'

Domenico stared back at her, looking stunned and momentarily lost for words, and Rae enjoyed the ripples of her victory, because not many people could render Domenico Ricci speechless.

He composed himself within a few seconds, however, and an echo of a smile played at the edges of his too sensual mouth as he responded. '*Bene.* You will go to London.' Rae opened her mouth to tell him that she had neither asked for nor required his permission, but he held up a hand and continued in his low, silken drawl. 'However, you won't be going alone. I'll accompany you,' he asserted, reaching out to tug her closer, into the shadow cast by his body, until there was very little space separating them, 'because, *cara*, the masquerade starts now.'

CHAPTER FOUR

THE RICCI PRIVATE JET touched down in London the following morning. On Domenico's instruction a car was waiting on the tarmac to drive them to the luxurious central hotel in which he had reserved a suite and they passed the drive through the capital in the same way they had spent the flight from Venice—in silence.

Domenico had plenty of things he could say, but he refused to give Rae the satisfaction of knowing how deeply her departure four months ago had bothered him. So he'd bitten his tongue and busied himself with work, fighting the rising urge to sit back, rest his eyes on her in the seat opposite and enjoy all the loveliness of her the way he often used to.

In her simple outfit of jeans, plain tee and well-worn leather jacket she looked beautiful, and he loathed her for it. Loathed the way the clothes hugged her slender figure, highlighting her hourglass curves and making him desperate to run his hands over them. Loathed how her freshly washed hair shone and curled over her shoulders, calling to him to once again bury his fingers in its lustrous length, to curl it around his hand

and gently tilt her head back until her mouth was ripe to receive his kiss.

Once in the car, Domenico stared out of the window rather than look at her, but every so often her reflection would appear in the dark glass and he would tense at the onslaught of longing stirred by her full lips and piercing eyes. It would be so easy to reach across and haul her onto his lap, he ruminated, to grind his groin against her and settle the ache hammering there, and it bothered him how large the idea loomed in his mind and how excited by it his body became.

Why did he continue to suffer this infernal attraction to her? Imagining all the ways he could drive her to make those delicious mewls of delight he so loved, and all the ways she could enchant him with her hands and lips and tongue. Rae had made it clear she had no love or respect for him. And that inequality of feeling infuriated him, stirring memories of another time he had yearned for something with every bone in his body... and the crushing rejection that had followed.

He'd always been fascinated by the idea of his mother. Elena had shielded him from the truth of how she came to raise him, simply telling him that his mother had had to leave him in her care, and so as a young, vividly imaginative boy he'd built a thousand scenarios around that mysterious mother figure, imagining all the possible reasons why she'd had to leave him and how it would be when she returned. When he'd finally learned her identity and seen a photograph of her she'd been even more beautiful than he'd imagined and, with a real face to revolve around, his daydreams had grown even grander.

When he'd heard she was in Venice, those dreams had seemed on the verge of coming true. He'd been sure that she was there for him. To see him. Claim him. But when they had finally come face to face, she'd shown none of the joy that he'd dreamt of. Her eyes, when they had finally come to rest on him, had turned cold and cruel, before she turned her face away, as though she didn't know him at all.

The incident had left him crushed and reeling, but he'd been too foolish, too full of hope, to learn his lesson and he'd gone to find her at her home. He had begged, he remembered with nauseating clarity, for a moment of her time, a conversation, that was all, but the rejection had been swift and brutal. The look that chased him away had told him he was nothing. Less than nothing. It was a look that, until Rae, had prevented him from ever getting too close to anyone.

However, he was older now. Wiser. And this situation with Rae would not be the same, he reassured himself. He was capable of ignoring the inclinations of his body and the messages being telegraphed by his recklessly beating heart, and even more reckless libido. All he wanted from her was her cooperation to ensure he inherited Palazzo Ricci. He harboured no hopes and he would not be *begging* for anything.

That was Domenico's last thought before they pulled up outside the hotel. They were checked in quickly, his name prompting a flurry of activity, but as soon as they entered the confined space of the elevator, Rae's gentle scent hit him like a punch, making him question that resolve as it took him right back to their most intimate moments, when he was deep inside her and the world began and ended with her. To the way she moved atop him, covering his body with her own, silencing his groans with kisses, fogging his mind with that light-as-air scent—*her* scent.

The moment they entered the suite he strode over to the terrace doors and pushed them open, partly to assess the view but mostly to flood the room with clean spring air and dilute the potency of her presence. Feeling fatigued, though it was only just past noon, Domenico availed himself of the top-of-the-line coffee machine and then carried his very strong espresso out onto the terrace. He was sipping at his coffee when he noticed Rae emerging from the far side of the suite and heading for the door, her jacket on and bag hanging from her shoulder.

'Are you going somewhere?' he demanded, quickly stalking back indoors.

She flashed him a look that said it was obvious. 'To do what I came here to do. Press pause on my life for the next six months.' Turning her back on him, she reached for the door handle. 'I'll be back in a while.'

'That's a little vague for my liking, Rae.'

Her shoulders stiffened and Domenico had the distinct impression she was counting to three and taking a deep breath before responding. Not for the first time, he caught himself reflecting that she was much spikier than she'd been before. Quicker to argue and sharper with her retorts. Thinking back to the way she had challenged him about the particulars of her return, forcing him to hastily rearrange his schedule to accompany her to London, he couldn't say he appreciated the argumentativeness but, for reasons unknown to him, he was somewhat intrigued by her new gutsy spirit. He wondered where she'd been hiding it throughout their marriage.

'I'm going to hand in my notice at work and then I'm going home to see my sisters and to pack up my things.'

Domenico searched her expression for any sign of deceit, though he wasn't sure he trusted himself to recognise it. She had, after all, fooled him for a long number of months into thinking that she was as invested in their marriage as he was.

'Very well.' He set down his cup and reached for his phone. 'I'll call for the car.'

'I don't need the car.'

'You may feel like traipsing across London with luggage. I, however, do not.'

'Since you're not coming with me, I don't see why what *you* feel like is relevant,' she riposted with a flash of temper, crossing her arms defensively over her chest, which was rising and falling with each flustered breath. Much to his frustration, the movement only drew his attention to the generous shape of her breasts beneath her shirt and abruptly all he could think about was how responsive they'd been to his touch. How Rae had loved him to flick and lick and suck. How she would writhe beneath him and beg breathlessly for him to keep going.

'It's relevant because I *am* coming with you,' he snapped, breaking free from those thoughts, but only with great effort.

Outrage glowed in her eyes like sudden flames, enhancing their naturally bright hue. 'No.'

'Yes.' Lifting his jacket from the back of the chair, he pulled it on.

'I don't need an escort, Domenico.' When he didn't bother to respond to her jibe, she huffed out an irritated sigh. 'I gave you my word that I would go through with this charade. So what is it that you think I'm going to do? Disappear into the crowds of the city and never be seen again?'

'No, I don't think that's going to happen,' he responded, rapidly losing patience, 'because I'm not going to allow it. You may have given your word, Rae, but surely you can understand why it doesn't count for much.'

He might be foolish enough to still desire her, but he was not such a fool that he would trust her ever again. Not after what she had done.

So he would not be letting her out of his sight, at least not until she had proven herself. And on one level he was curious about the life she had chosen over him. Masochistically eager to see what had been so much more worthwhile than him. Than *them*.

'So,' he said, forcing himself to ignore the hurt clawing its way into her gaze and gesturing for her to precede him out of the door. 'After you.'

So this was what she had left him for.

It was the sole thought in Domenico's head as the car pulled away from the kerb outside the bistro in her home suburb of Wandsworth, where Rae had seemingly been working, and set off towards her house.

To be a hostess in a high street restaurant and live back in the house she had grown up in with her sisters.

It was unfathomable! He could give her the world and she had picked this?

Turning his face away from the window with a barely suppressed breath of anger, he dug his phone from his inner jacket pocket and with a frustrated jab accessed his emails, questioning afresh how he had made such an error in judgement in granting Rae access to his life. That he had ever considered her different from the women from his past was perplexing to him now, and there was little comfort in recognising that she had fooled Elena just as convincingly.

His aunt had often remarked that she thought Rae possessed a similar spirit to her own, but Rae's actions had thoroughly debunked that. Elena had been one of the wisest, kindest, most loyal people he'd ever known. She had never turned her back on him, or anyone in need, and although Domenico sometimes questioned if she had only taken him in to fill her barren life after her husband Raphael's premature death, and to give herself a once longed-for heir, he'd never doubted her affection for him.

However, it was that ugly question that drove him to work so hard, to build The Ricci Group—Raphael's business—into something even bigger than Raphael Ricci or Elena had dreamed of. To prove to Elena that she had been right to take him in when no one else had wanted him. To show her that, out of all the lost boys in the world, he was deserving of the good fortune she'd bestowed on him. Even if *he* never quite felt deserving of it, of the love and attention she had offered.

It was as though his abandonment as a newborn baby had stained him, marking him out as unwanted, and nothing he did, however hard he worked or how much he gave, could erase that mark, or the feeling that sometimes crawled beneath his skin because of it.

It was a feeling not helped by the world he inhabited, where it was never clear if the people who flocked to his side and fussed and flirted in the hope of earning his favour did so because they actually wanted to know him, or because they could not resist the lure of his wealth and status.

He'd never had that concern with Rae. Whilst instantly recognisable in Italy and other countries across the Continent, his profile in England had been relatively low when they'd met. Rae had known nothing of his wealth or the Ricci name. Her interest had been solely in Domenico, the man. For a short while, at least, and when that had waned, even the wealth and luxury he could offer hadn't been enough of an incentive to cajole her into staying.

She just hadn't wanted him. Like so many others before her.

He hated that it hurt him, like a scalpel splitting his skin open and tearing it back so he felt exposed. Vulnerable. Domenico thought he had excised all those feelings long ago. Whatever small splinters had remained had been dealt with in the aftermath of Rae's departure, plucked out like thorns. But he could feel a fresh spill of that poison, spreading outwards and infecting his thoughts and his mood, propelling him back to that day when he had stood in the freezing, pouring rain, pleading for the chance to know his family, only to have the door slammed in his face.

It was a memory, and an insecurity, that he couldn't abide and he loathed Rae for stirring it up, for making him feel weak, especially when he had been a damn good husband to her.

As his wife she had wanted for nothing. She hadn't needed to work. She'd had the freedom to travel with him in opulence and comfort to the most exciting cities the world had to offer and to enjoy them in a luxurious manner that most people could only dream of.

Her only responsibilities—if they could even be called that—had been to represent their family and business with poise and elegance. To attend the necessary social functions and work with certain charitable organisations and, every so often, coordinate with a team of event planners to set up a party on behalf of The Ricci Group.

What cause had she had to leave?

The life flying past on the other side of the window was the life Rae had left behind to be with him in the first place. And she had left it easily, happily. So why had she returned to it? It could only be that she'd stopped loving him.

That he hadn't been enough.

The story of his life.

But she had been as close to capitulating to the swirling fire between them as he had, and didn't that indicate that she felt something for him? That he continued to hold some mastery over her emotions?

In which case...

Basta!

Enough!

Vexed by that dangerous train of thought because it was contaminated with too much hope, Domenico ruthlessly shut down those thoughts. It didn't matter why Rae had left, only that she had. Even if he was able to burrow inside her mind and understand her ultimate reasoning, what would it change? There was no going back for them. She had betrayed him. Broken his trust. Broken everything they had built together. So he resolved to give it no more thought, and focus only on the issues that could be resolved—like his inheritance.

Rae was beyond relieved when the car pulled up outside her family home on the tree-lined residential street in Wandsworth and she was able to escape the confines of the car and with it the intoxicating, darkly sweet scent of Domenico's supremely male body and the feel of that body so close to her.

'Do you want to come in?' she offered out of politeness.

'No. I'll wait here for you. I have more emails that I need to respond to and you probably need some private time with your sisters.'

She tried not to show her relief. After the flight, which had seemed to take double the normal time, and crisscrossing the capital in midday traffic, Rae badly needed a reprieve, and not just from her bodily reactions to him, but the disapproval that had been radiating off him in violent waves ever since realising she'd taken a part-time job as a hostess and waitress at a local restaurant. Domenico had taken one look at the frontage of the bistro and his lips had instantly compressed together in that flat line that expressed his discontent. Senior executives at Ricci lived in fear of that compression of his mouth, but Rae had only ever been subjected to it on occasion, most memorably the once or twice that she had tried to express a preference that she did not accompany him to a particular event.

Using her key to let herself into the house, Rae hadn't even shut the door before she was set upon by her sisters, demanding the answers she hadn't been willing to give them during the brief call she had made from Venice. Sitting with them in the living room, she slowly explained all that had unfolded and what would happen next.

'So you're actually going back to Venice to live with him and pretend you are still together for the next six months?' Maggie demanded in open-mouthed disbelief. 'Have you completely lost your mind?' she exploded.

'Maggie!' Imogen chided.

'Don't Maggie me!' she fired at their youngest sister. 'It's absurd and if you're being honest, you think it is too.'

'I know it's crazy,' Rae admitted, looking between her sisters. 'But helping him is the right thing to do. For him, and for me too.' By their looks of scepticism, she knew she needed to explain further. 'I want to draw a line underneath this whole chapter. I've got so many good things to look forward to, but Domenico is always lurking at the back of my mind. There's no closure there and I know the only way I'm going to be able to get that is by going back and proving that I've learned something about myself. That I've changed and I'm not going to make the same mistakes again.'

'Rae, how can you even think that? You're so different from the person you were when you were married to Domenico. Both Imogen and I see it,' Maggie reassured her urgently.

'Totally,' Imogen agreed quickly. 'You're more assertive, you have such a determined focus on your bridal collection, you're chasing it with everything you've got. We're so impressed by what you're doing and we're so proud of you.'

'You saying that means a lot,' she said, taking both her sisters' hands in hers. 'But this is just something I need to do. For myself.'

'Then do it,' Imogen said, squeezing her hand. 'We're here for you whatever.'

Content with the support of her sisters, Rae went upstairs to begin the task of packing her clothes. From the window of her bedroom that overlooked the street she could see Domenico's car outside. She could make out his figure in the back seat, gesturing with his free hand as he spoke on the phone, and the movements were so familiar to her that her heart gave a kick and nervousness fluttered deep inside her chest.

Six months, she reminded herself. *That's all. You can do this. There's nothing to be nervous about. You'll prove exactly how much you've changed, that you're ca-*

pable of being around him and not sacrificing anything of yourself. That you don't have to suffer the way Mum did. And then you can walk away with a clear conscience and an even bigger belief in yourself.

Buoyed by that pep talk, Rae spun away from the window and reached for her case, because the sooner she got the ordeal started, the sooner she'd be on the other side of it and that wonderful, exhilarating, heart-breaking, petrifying chapter of her life with Domenico would be over for good.

CHAPTER FIVE

RAE HADN'T BEEN back in Venice a full three days when Domenico informed her that they would be attending a black-tie ball at the end of the week. He had given her fair warning it was what he expected and Rae knew she had agreed to it, but still the prospect of attending a function on his arm had her heart racing and chest constricting. It wasn't just that there would be dozens of sets of eyes on them, all watching to be convinced of the continued validity of their union; it was that there would be no escape from Domenico.

In the days that she had been back in Venice, Rae had seen him only a handful of times. He was staying true to his word about living separate lives in private, and that suited her just fine. She was able to devote her alone time to her bridal design business, working on new ideas as well as her ongoing orders, and when she needed a break she would take a leisurely wander of the city that had long ago captured her heart, strolling along the narrow waterways or enjoying the bustling piazzas from outside a coffee shop. However, that lack of contact or communication in private created a greater nervousness about being with him in public, because they were going from one extreme to another. From zero interaction to pretending to be in love.

Obviously, she had realised when she'd agreed to return that the pretence would be necessary, but she'd been so preoccupied with her emotions about returning that she hadn't given much—*any*—thought to the practicalities of it.

But now all Rae could think about was all the ways Domenico would be touching and holding her.

How he would casually drape an arm around her shoulders or her waist, stroke his fingertip across her cheek, brush escaped tendrils of hair from her face, all with a gentleness of touch that was at odds with his brute size and that provoked a seismic reaction beneath her skin. And he would probably kiss her, holding her captive beneath that dark chocolate gaze before slowly, so her anticipation built, lowering his lips until they met hers in an eruption of quiet, screaming passion.

As she imagined it all in excruciating slow motion, something rippled across her skin—something Rae wanted to pretend she hadn't felt or recognised. Because to give a name to it would make it real and she didn't want it to be real. Couldn't let it be real. Not if she was going to emerge intact at the end of their six-month arrangement.

Despite her unease, on the allotted night she was dressed in her finery and descending the palazzo's long curved staircase to meet Domenico. Although he had given her a new credit card to cover all of her costs, Rae had selected a dress from her old wardrobe, a previously unworn classic creation of black silk from a renowned

Italian designer that floated around her like air. The straps were thin and delicate and the design cut very low on her back, showing more skin than she ideally wanted to display, but it had been the only black dress amongst her existing collection. She had set her mind on wearing black, hoping it would attract less attention than a bolder hue, not that it really mattered when Domenico always attracted so much attention, never mind with the addition of all sorts of swirling rumours...

He was waiting for her at the bottom of the staircase, his back to her, and her heart stopped at the sight of his broad back, sheathed in the pristine fabric of the expertly fitted tuxedo. It showed to perfection the raw strength of his body and Rae found herself gripping the banister for support as her knees suddenly felt too weak to keep holding her up.

Naked, he was mesmerising, a mouthwatering specimen to behold, but Rae had always thought that he was as much of a sensation clothed and the thrill of him in that moment did nothing to dispel that opinion. One of her favourite things about evenings when they'd attended some fancy soirée had been knowing that at the end of the night her hands would have the privilege of sliding the fine clothes from his body to find the hot skin beneath. Not that she had that privilege any more, or that she wanted it, she reminded herself sharply, hurrying the final few steps as though she could leave those feelings behind her.

Hearing the click of her heels against the floor, Domenico spun around, his eyes crashing into hers. Rae swallowed as his glittering gaze swept over her, his jaw tightening fractionally though he offered no comment.

'You should wear this too,' he said, turning to the table behind him and lifting a velvet box that, when he popped it open, revealed a diamond choker.

'That was Elena's,' Rae breathed, stunned that he was presenting it to her.

'Yes. A much-admired piece of her collection. She wore it often, and you wearing it tonight should signal that everything in our marriage is perfect. I would hardly let someone I didn't love and was estranged from wear something so precious, would I?'

Rae swallowed again, unable to read beneath the hard glint of his richly dark eyes or the silkily lethal drawl of his words. But his willingness to allow her to wear such a priceless heirloom reminded her just how important this charade was to him and, as much as she wanted to refuse, she knew it wouldn't be a wise way to start the evening and so simply turned as he lifted the jewels from the box.

With deft fingers he fastened it around her neck, his hot fingers brushing her trembling flesh. The quivers racing over her skin sank even deeper into her and for the second time in as many minutes she thought her legs were about to give way. And it didn't help that he was standing so close that Rae could feel all the strength and heat of his body and she so badly wanted to press back against it, to feel the power of him enveloping her once more.

Domenico moved her by the shoulders so she was standing before an antique mirror.

'What do you think?' he asked, his dark eyes so steadily fixed on hers that he would see anything she felt.

Slowly, Rae met his gaze and, as she did, feeling throbbed in every inch of her. 'It's stunning.'

Their eyes held and her breath grew shallower. Could he feel it too? That pulse of passion and longing streaming between them. There seemed to be a million thoughts and feelings locked in the darkness of his gaze—emotions he had no intention of giving voice to. But Rae couldn't speak either, strangled by the heavy emotion coursing through her, thudding hotly in her sex in a beat that refused to be ignored.

She frantically searched his face with her eyes, wanting some sign that his blood was running as hot as hers, scared by the thought that it was and equally scared that it wasn't.

'We should go,' he said, stepping back easily and moving towards the front door.

Her skin instantly chilled, though her blood still ran hot and she cursed her stupidity. If she couldn't even *stand* close to him without turning into a puddle, what would it be like when he actually did touch her? The last thing she wanted was a repeat of what had almost happened in the upstairs corridor the night of Elena's funeral, when she'd gone up in sizzling flames at the barest of touches. The only way to keep that from happening, Rae realised, was to set some boundaries. *Now.*

'Before we go...' Rae began, seizing the moment to assert her will in a way she never would have thought to previously. 'I know everyone needs to believe that we are madly in love, but I was thinking we should establish some ground rules.'

Domenico arched a brow. 'Such as?'

'I know we need to be affectionate with one another and that's fine. But within reason. So I would prefer it if we didn't kiss on the mouth,' she specified assertively. 'It's not unreasonable, I think. Many other couples restrain from such displays in public.'

'I don't recall us being one of those couples,' he drawled, evidently finding the idea ridiculous, and he wasn't wrong. They'd never succeeded in keeping their hands off one another, but Rae had also never previously imposed her will on their relationship and look at her now. She was proof that things could change.

Holding herself steady beneath his unflinching regard, because she knew that he was expecting her to back down, she said in a controlled voice, 'I have faith that we can convince people we're happy without being overt in our displays of affection.'

'Hmm. Fine,' he agreed, his jaw locked tight. 'We'll keep kissing off the agenda for the evening. But let's make sure everything else is convincing, *si*?' he added with a look of warning. 'Vincenzo D'Aragona is still in the city and it's likely he too will be attending tonight.'

Rae nodded, that tiny lump in her throat tripling in size. As if she hadn't felt enough pressure without knowing their judge and jury would there too!

The ballroom was full of people by the time they arrived and as they walked through the doors Domenico clasped her hand tightly in his. Rae wished it didn't feel so good, so right, to have his strong fingers wrapped around hers, to be claimed as his again. As expected, all eyes followed their arrival and beneath her beautiful dress Rae's heart thrashed against the cage of her ribs.

She tried to focus instead on the opulence of the venue. The high ceiling, the trio of glittering chandeliers, the string orchestra arranged in one corner and mammoth vases of fragrant flowers delineating the perimeter of the room.

She and Domenico exchanged polite greetings with many of the couples in attendance before collecting drinks from the bar and standing at one of the high top tables. Rae was able to breathe for all of two seconds before she spied renowned socialite Luisa D'Amato strutting in their direction, her sights very much fixed on them. Behind her smile Rae's teeth gritted together, her body tightening even more. Luisa was the very last person she wanted to deal with. Their interactions had always been unpleasant, with every single remark she'd ever made designed to make Rae feel small and insecure and incompetent, and as hard as Rae had tried to withstand their power, they'd somehow always left their mark, chipping at her confidence and her sense of security as Domenico's wife. Not that Domenico had ever noticed, and Rae had never raised it with him, not wanting to appear petty or insecure, or as if she couldn't handle herself in his world. But it had just become one more pretence, one more truth she wasn't speaking, and one more brick in that ever-growing wall between them.

'Rae, so wonderful to have you back,' Luisa trilled as she reached them, air kissing each of her cheeks.

'It's lovely to be back,' Rae replied with a smile.

Luisa surveyed her through heavily made-up eyes. 'I must admit, we were starting to wonder if we would ever see you again, you were gone for so long. If only you'd heard some of the rumours going around,' she murmured, leaning in almost conspiratorially. 'That perhaps your marriage was over. Absolutely crazy, I said. But that's why it's dangerous to leave one's husband unattended for so long. Hopes, as I'm sure you can understand, were getting rather high. But I assure you, Rae, I did my best to keep some of the more predatory women away. No doubt you can imagine who I'm talking about,' she went on, gesturing not so subtly with her eyes to a passing female. 'But I suppose it's always nice to know you have options,' she added with a direct look of smiling suggestion at Domenico, 'should you ever want them.'

Rae's fingers clenched dangerously around the crystal flute of champagne in her hand, unable to believe what Luisa had just said, and yet not surprised at all. But after all the catty remarks and slights Rae had had to suffer from her, that was too blatantly disrespectful, too far over the line, and she wasn't going to just quietly accept it the way she always had before.

Throwing back her shoulders, she met Luisa's gaze. 'I'm very grateful for your help, Luisa, although I knew I had nothing to worry about. It's not as though anyone here is Domenico's type or he wouldn't have still been single when I came along, would he?' she mused, trailing a hand down his arm. 'But your care and attention towards him is much appreciated, especially when you could have been using that time to look for husband number three. Or it is number four? I've lost track.'

From the corner of her eye Rae was sure she caught Domenico's look of surprise, but she was more interested in Luisa's faltering expression.

'If you'll excuse me, I see Antonia and I need to speak with her. But it is wonderful to see you.'

'You too. Say hello from me.' Rae smiled as Luisa walked away. A small sense of satisfaction rippled through her, but she hated that she'd earned it by engaging in the same unkindness that Luisa practised.

'Are you okay?' Domenico asked in her ear, a low whisper that sent shivers rippling through her.

'I'm fine,' she replied, taking a sip of her champagne in the hope of shedding the nasty feeling snaking through her veins.

'Your hand is shaking, Rae.'

She looked at her hand to see Domenico was right, and then quickly up at him. 'I've never found Luisa to be the easiest person to deal with, that's all.'

He said nothing else, but placed a warm hand on the bare skin of her back, rubbing his palm up and down her spine, and within seconds she could feel the tension start to ease and her body begin to relax. Whether Domenico had intended it as an act of comfort and reassurance or as a necessary show of affection, Rae wasn't sure, and the answer did not prove forthcoming as her awareness narrowed to that mesmerising motion of his hand over her sensitive skin, streams of hot, sparkly feeling running in a dozen different directions.

She wanted that delicious feeling in the rest of her

body too. She wanted those clever fingers to slide up her spine and graze her side. Wanted them to slip beneath the silk and curl over her breast, for him to touch and tease as he'd once loved to, and as she'd loved also. How many times had he brought her to screaming orgasm just by lavishing the hot attention of his lips and tongue on her breasts?

The bliss of imagining was dashed as she felt eyes scalding her skin. Across the ballroom, Luisa and her group of friends stared their way, murmuring intently amongst themselves.

'Ignore them.' Domenico's lips were against her ear again, his hand continuing to trace over her skin, skating a line up and down her spine.

'She's ghastly... To stand there and say those things to my face.' Rae looked up at him. His expression was unconcerned and that rattled her even more, breath hissing from between her lips. 'Not that I expect you to care. You're probably delighted to know you have so many options.'

His eyes gleamed, dark and rich and completely devastating. 'A little late to be possessive, isn't it?' he remarked with a slight smile, sliding his hand to the curve of her waist and pulling her even tighter against his muscled body, and she hated that it did make her feel better. That each caress softened her mood that little bit more. That the nearer she was to his body, the more the rest of the room seemed to slide away. 'You never seemed to be bothered by the women and their comments before.'

Was he actually that obtuse? Rae thought with a frowning glance up at him. Or had her feelings really mattered so little to him that he'd never spared a thought for how those high society social occasions, in which she had no experience, could be difficult for her? It was hardly a new realisation, but it was jarring all the same.

'Of course I was bothered by them, Domenico,' she sighed, frustration loosening her tongue.

The look on his face was one she recognised: he was chewing over that information, trying to fit it in with all that he already knew. 'You never said anything.'

The words contained a mild accusation and Rae moved her shoulders in a small inexpressive shrug. She was regretting having said anything about it now and making it a bigger deal, highlighting her silly female feelings when she'd only ever wanted him to think of her as strong and capable, the perfect wife. The weight of his stare was unmoving, though, and Rae knew she had to say something to defuse the heaviness of the moment and diminish her confession.

'Most of the time there didn't seem to be much point in complaining about it,' she admitted reluctantly and uncomfortably. 'It's not like it's something you can control, Domenico. I just saw it as a reality of being with you. Of course other women were going to be catty or jealous or mean. You're a beautiful man. You're wealthy. You're powerful. One of those is catnip. All three together is a lethal combination. Naturally, any woman who looks at you is going to find you irresistible. Because you are.'

His hand had stopped moving. He stared down at her, a new light moving through his powerful gaze and, much to her annoyance, Rae realised she had done the opposite of what she'd wanted. Instead of brushing him off, she'd only made him want to dig deeper into her feelings. 'Irresistible?'

He repeated the word with a quirk of his lips and for the barest of seconds he looked like the Domenico she was used to—the Domenico she'd fallen head over heels for and married in a whirlwind. Charismatic and quick-minded, with that devastating slash of a smile. There was none of the cool distance, none of the well-bred politeness he'd treated her with on their few brief encounters since she'd been back.

'It's only the truth,' Rae replied huskily, feeling colour rush to her cheeks as she cursed herself for giving away something else that she shouldn't have. For giving him a first-hand look at the feelings she was alternating between ignoring and denying.

Domenico seemed to be on the verge of saying something else, his eyes dark with thoughts, before clearly changing his mind. 'We should dance,' he said instead, prising her flute from her hand and leading her to the centre of the room, where many couples were already taking advantage of the lilting music to move in smooth circles around the floor.

Domenico pulled her in close. His jaw brushed her cheek, the touch jolting through her like an electric shock. She caught the scent of him, strong and sharp, and it clouded her head completely and Rae had to fight the urge to brush her lips across his smooth, sweet-smelling skin, to sample his flesh with the tip of her tongue.

Get a grip, Rae.

This was only the first of many public outings that would demand their closeness. If she was going to simmer with unwanted desire each time, it was going to be a very long six months. She had to figure out a way to control herself. Had to remember that for all the reasons Domenico was right, he was also very, *very* wrong for her.

They imagined different futures. He wanted a wife permanently at his side and she wanted, *needed*, a life of her own.

Engaging in anything remotely physical, even entertaining thoughts of such caresses, would only muddy the waters and it would be far better for them both if they stayed unmuddied.

But as he moved her effortlessly across the floor, Rae's body continued to purr under their tempting closeness and the expert press of his hands against her flesh. His touch had always been her undoing and Rae could feel it starting to occur again, that unravelling of herself as her body slowly surrendered to his compelling touch of possession.

Had it not been for the eyes continuing to follow them, primarily Luisa and her friends, Rae would have drifted off entirely, but their predatory watchfulness kept her rooted in reality, their hard and hungry gazes making her stomach writhe and twist.

Because Luisa had been right. Domenico did have options, plenty of them. There was a queue of women waiting for a chance to be with him and once their charade was over, once it became public knowledge that their marriage was dead, a few of them would probably get that chance.

If they hadn't already.

That sudden burst of thought had tears pressing up against her eyes and an inexplicable emotion gushing through her and sticking at the back of her throat. She knew, however, that was how they wanted her to feel, insecure and vulnerable. It was the way she'd often felt at these events and around these ruthless, predatory women. But, as far as they were concerned, Domenico was still hers.

And her only job tonight was to show exactly how much he did belong to her, how his heart beat for her and his body hungered for her.

Only her.

Twisting her face inwards, the tip of her nose glided along his smooth, tanned jaw and Rae allowed herself to succumb to the scent of him, dark and strong. Playing along, Domenico tipped his head down, his lips within easy reach, just like that night in the hallway, but, unlike that night, Rae didn't hesitate, extending her neck so that their mouths met.

That first feather-light brush of their lips was shattering. He tasted better than she'd allowed herself to remember. Like desire and hope and passion. The gentle motion of their mouths changed as her hands slid up his powerfully muscled chest and curled around his neck. The answering press of his lips became harder, his mouth shaping to hers with more ferocity, seeking more of her passion, which she eagerly gave. Domenico held her more securely, the band of his arms around her back crushing her breasts to the solid expanse of his chest, and Rae very nearly melted, having forgotten just how amazing it felt to be held against the broad wall of beating flesh. As if nothing could hurt her ever again. As if there was no safer place for her in the whole world.

The heat crackling between them could have burned her dress right off her body and Rae didn't know if it was his heart or her own that she could feel racing. But she knew she wanted the kiss. Wanted it with every catch of her breath and every flutter of her pulse. Wanted it more than she remembered ever wanting any kiss, and she didn't want it to prove something, but wanted it for herself.

It was Domenico who drew back first, keeping tight hold and staring down at her, his eyes alight. 'What happened to your ground rules?' he demanded huskily.

Good question, Rae thought, feeling intoxicated, her mind fuzzy.

'It seemed necessary,' she lied, the words coming too slow. 'We were being watched. And I was under orders to be convincing, was I not?'

His eyes flashed as if he found her answer provocative somehow, and his face adopted the set expression that preceded an interrogation that always got him the answers he wanted. But then it was gone and he was drawing back and leading her from the dancefloor.

'I think that's enough for tonight,' he said as the music ended. 'We'll leave now.'

She blinked with surprise. 'But we've not been here that long.'

'Long enough,' he countered. 'And after that kiss, no

one will find our departure strange. Everyone will assume we're in a hurry to get home and continue our reunion.'

Rae's cheeks flamed. But that was exactly what the kiss had felt like so it had most certainly looked just as passionate. Burning with mortification, she let Domenico take her hand and lead her from the ballroom, but, as soon as she could, she pulled her hand free. She said nothing on the journey back to the palazzo and, once they arrived, she ran up the stairs, tossing a hurried goodnight over her shoulder.

Domenico watched Rae fly up the stairs, his mouth still tingling with the incendiary passion of that brief kiss. The taste of her remained on his lips and the fever she had stirred in his blood with her unrestrained hunger continued to scorch his veins.

He had been doing his best to keep his attraction contained behind bolted doors, to avoid any repeat of the lapse that had happened the night of Elena's funeral, but with that unexpected kiss she had blasted the doors wide open, allowing the scorching desire to stream through him unchecked, and all he wanted to do was continue what she had started.

Wanted to tease her mouth with his, suck her lower lip between her teeth. Wanted to slide the black silk from her body and see with his own eyes what she wore beneath. Wanted to hear her whimpers, then her pleas and then her screams as he drove her towards blissful oblivion.

He wanted everything he had tasted in that kiss and, before he knew what he was doing, Domenico was following her up the stairs, taking them two at a time, his feet keeping pace with the roaring and pounding of his blood.

Reaching her door, Domenico wrapped his fingers around the handle...only to suddenly stop.

Because suddenly he was outside a house and the door was being opened and the eyes staring back at him turned to the coldest stone when he stated who he was. And then, as if the words spoken hadn't been cruel enough, the door was being shut in his face.

A cold sweat dampening the back of his neck, Domenico released the handle and backed away from the door.

She could spurn his advance, deny the fire that had powered that kiss. Reject him. And he could not bear that. Not again, and not from her.

So he would ignore it. He would drag every last drop of feeling back under his control, close those doors and seal them with an extra bolt. He would bury that desire beneath pragmatism, smother the flames with the memory of her betrayal and keep himself safe from another stinging rejection.

CHAPTER SIX

ANOTHER NIGHT, ANOTHER CHARADE.

They were attending the opening of a new restaurant overlooking the Grand Canal and being in such close proximity to Rae again, Domenico was once more struggling to keep control of himself.

In a fitted blue dress paired with open-toed stilettoes and a black leather jacket draped across her shoulders as there was a chill to the evening air and they were seated outside, Rae looked sensational. His heart had struck up a restless beat the moment he'd locked eyes on her back at the palazzo, a dizzying cocktail of heat and need moving through his blood and making his heart race and it hadn't stopped since. In the pearlescent glow from the low candles forming the centrepiece of the table, the alluring power of her vivid blue eyes was impossible to avoid and the fever stirring in his blood was only intensifying and there seemed to be nothing he could do about it. Nothing he could do to stop the sultry memories from cascading through his mind, one after the other, each more arousing than the last. Nothing to stop him thinking about how close he had been to charging into her suite and taking her in his arms the last time they'd been together and how he wasn't sure he had it in him to resist again.

In the days since their last public outing Domenico had barely seen her, not because of any special effort on his part but because his normal daily routine was so demanding. He rose early for a punishing workout before heading to his office, where it was customary to spend up to twelve hours, but, with the final pieces of a major deal still being worked out, those hours had been running closer and closer to midnight. By the time he returned to the palazzo most nights Rae had eaten dinner alone and was secluded in her suite, and though that lack of interaction had not been by design, Domenico was relieved by it.

Because he didn't trust himself around her at all. All it took was for him to catch her scent in the air and need unfurled within him like a fast-flowing river, and he hated the thought of being so tempted by her that he abandoned his good sense. That he forgot the lessons he'd paid so dearly to learn.

All he needed was her presence, her cooperation—for her to stick around for the next six months so he could retain ownership of what was already rightfully his. He required nothing else, not from her.

But even knowing that, even having told himself that every day since Rae had been back in Venice, he could not keep his eyes from devouring her or his thoughts from dwelling with heightened awareness on all the ways she was so very different from the woman he had married.

There was an aura of self-possession to her now that

had been absent before. He could see it just by looking at her, in the way her shoulders were thrown back, her head held high. She refused to be intimidated by anyone or anything, and had proven that at the ball a few nights previously, when she'd handled Luisa's catty remarks with a cutting comeback of her own. Luisa had thoroughly deserved it and seeing her slammed back into her box had been satisfying, but it had startled him to hear Rae being so sharp with her words. But an even greater source of consternation was that Rae had felt she'd had to respond in such a way. Because her reaction had made it obvious that she'd suffered Luisa's unpleasantness in the past too, and that she had been wounded by it, and he had never known.

And he should have.

He should have noticed and taken action to protect her. Rae was his wife. He had brought her into his life and his world and it had been his responsibility to take care of and defend her. Only he clearly hadn't, and because of that failing Rae had been forced to act out of character, and that was not sitting well with him at all.

Not that he didn't appreciate her newfound strength and confidence. That flare of fire in her eyes when she'd refused to back down, and the steely determination to get her own way, even when up against his powerful will, were definitely intriguing new facets of her, but where those changes had sprung from and why she'd felt the need to change were questions running on a loop in his mind. Testing and troubling him. Driving him to question if he had paid enough attention, if he'd worked hard enough to discover exactly what had been swirling beneath the serene façade she had presented to him. After all, he hadn't known about her unease around Luisa, or how sensitive she'd been to the cruel society gossip. What else had he been unaware of? What else had he missed?

'How's your food?' Rae asked, seeing that he wasn't eating as his thoughts wandered.

He reached for his wine glass, taking a sip of the rich merlot to moisten his bone-dry mouth, and loosen the intensity of his single-track thoughts. 'It's good. You'll like it. Here, try a little.'

Domenico held out his fork to her, knowing it painted the picture of a devoted husband, but as her lips tightened around the fork and it slid between her mouth, he realised his mistake, realised that he had just poured oil on the fire simmering in his blood and, right on cue, he felt it, that sudden violent strain against his trousers. And as he imagined those perfectly ripe lips clamped around his throbbing length, sucking him deeper into the warm wetness of her mouth, his erection only grew more solid. More excruciating.

Heat raced along his veins, his skin suddenly too tight for his body as he worked to block out the erotic image in order to block the feelings it conjured, but it was too vivid, too potent. Hard as he tried, Domenico couldn't loosen the fixed image from his mind and, far from steadying himself, a wild, reckless abandon was mounting in him, urging him to take Rae's hand, slide it beneath the table and onto his crotch. Nothing in that moment seemed more urgent than letting her feel exactly what she did to him, and reminding her what powerful pleasure he could offer her in return.

Knowing he needed to change the direction of his thoughts and *fast*—before he did something he would majorly regret later—he searched desperately through his hazy mind for a safe topic of conversation.

'You were speaking with Imogen earlier?' Rae had been speaking to her on the phone when he'd returned home to the palazzo. 'How is she?'

Rae stared back at him, her slim eyebrows halfway up her forehead.

'Why are you looking at me like that?'

'Because you hardly ever ask after my sisters,' Rae replied with her newly acquired bluntness.

'That's not true. I've asked about your sisters many times,' he insisted shortly, feeling defensive about the accusation because of course he'd asked about her sisters in the past. *Hadn't he?* 'And even if I didn't, I'm asking now.'

Rae softened her gaze and swallowed her small mouthful of food. 'She's good. She'd been at the library, studying for most of the day.'

'How is she getting on with her studies? Has she been enjoying her course?'

'Yes. She's doing really well.' Rae smiled, her pride in her youngest sister evident. 'Her classes finish at the end of the month. Then she has a few final assignments, but after that she'll focus on her dissertation. I want to try to coax her out here for a few weekends, get her away for a few days or she'll just work non-stop.'

Domenico watched her, seeing what she wasn't admitting in the pull of her lips and the concern momentarily clouding her beautiful eyes.

'You're worried about her?' Rae was always worried about Imogen and Maggie, but this was something else. 'Are you concerned she's pushing herself too much with her studies?'

'No. Well, yes, but it's not just that.' She offered no more, dropping her gaze and digging her fork back into her dish.

'We can't just sit here in silence, Rae. We need to talk about something. Imogen is a neutral topic at least,' he pointed out with cool pragmatism.

With a look that said she knew he had a point, she relented. 'Imogen got involved with someone last summer. I don't know who he was, I never met him and neither did Maggie. But she got in pretty deep with him pretty fast. And then he just walked away with barely more than a goodbye. Maggie and I didn't know about any of this until after it had happened, but it hit Ims hard. She became quiet, withdrawn. If she hadn't had her classes, I'm not sure she would have got out of bed.' Her forehead creased with a concerned frown. 'She's better now, a lot better, but I'm not sure she's completely over it.'

'A rejection like that, from someone she thought she could trust and who she thought she loved, she may never be completely over it. That kind of wound has a way of staying with you so that, even twenty years later, that sting of rejection feels just as sharp as the day it was inflicted,' Domenico imparted with all the certainty of someone who had experienced it himself and Rae's eyes lifted to his, the troubled blue of her gaze deepening to the colour of the darkest, deepest sea. It was that which alerted him to just how much he had inadvertently given away about himself. 'But she will move on. You just need to give her time. It doesn't happen overnight.'

Rae was still watching him, curiosity now burning in her gaze.

'What happened all those years ago that hurt you so badly, Domenico?' She leaned in closer, her eyes fixed on him with a compelling clarity and directness from which he felt there was no escape. 'You can tell me.'

'We were talking about Imogen,' he reminded her, growing more uncomfortable by the second under her intense gaze.

'Now I'm asking about you,' Rae responded. 'What happened? Who rejected you?'

Domenico looked off to the side. He had no intention of breaking his silence on the past. It was something he never talked about, but their conversation had unlocked an unpleasant memory that had started to snake through him and his usual tactic of pushing it aside was not working. In the strangest upending of emotion, he was struck by the desire to share it, to dispel it from his mind, and before he could examine that sudden urge, try to curb it, his lips were moving and he was answering her, information he had never spoken aloud before spilling out.

'My mother.' He faced Rae again. 'She lived here in Venice for a period when I was younger. By that time, I'd discovered who she was and when I found out that she was moving here I got so excited. I thought she had to be coming here because of me. *For me*. To see me, maybe have me come and live with her. It wasn't like I wanted to leave Elena—I loved her—but this was my mother. I'd been dreaming about meeting her for a long time.'

He paused, needing a moment, but the words were in a rush to escape. 'Every time the doorbell went during those days and weeks I leapt to my feet, so sure that it would be her. But it never was. She never came. Then one day Elena had taken me out for lunch and she was in the same restaurant. She walked straight past us and looked right at me. But, instead of smiling or stopping, she just looked right through me with those cold, hateful eyes and it was like I'd been burned. All I wanted to do was cry, but I didn't want to disappoint Elena, so I just held it in...'

Feeling emotion pressing at the backs of his eyes at the stinging recollection, Domenico shook his head, wanting to move on, erase that too intense moment. But looking across at Rae certainly didn't help. She was absorbed in all that new information. Having omitted all the finer details of his story, all she'd ever known about his childhood was that Elena had taken him in when his own mother had been unable to care for him. He'd never wanted her to know the whole ugly truth of how unwanted he'd been, fearful that with that knowledge she'd start to find him lacking too.

'But, like I said, Imogen will find a way to move on. She's strong. She'll be okay.'

Rae's eyes were stuck on him and he knew that, in spite of his attempt to draw attention back to her problem and her sister, Rae was thinking only of his story in that moment.

'How did *you* move on from that?'

Domenico was quiet for a second as he relived it, remembering the hurt and the confusion. Remembering how those emotions had spread through his body like a virus and how hard he'd fought against that anguish.

'I made the memory and feelings as small as I could and locked them in a little box where they could do no further harm,' he told her dispassionately.

Rae's hand had reached out and was curled around his fist, warm and soft, and the urge to twine his fingers through hers, to accept that comfort, was overwhelming.

'Did you ever see her again? Your mother.'

The lump in his throat was so large it was a second before he could answer. 'Only from afar.' But those sightings of her were tattooed into his brain too, because she hadn't been alone. She'd had her children with her—the children she had kept, the ones whose existence she had welcomed and celebrated. Whilst he'd remained ignored. 'And no,' he added more sharply than he intended as he anticipated her obvious follow-up question, 'she doesn't still live here. It's been years since I set eyes on her.'

'I'm sorry, Domenico. I don't know what to say other than that.'

'You don't need to say anything.'

He didn't need sympathetic words, or platitudes. He didn't need to talk about it. It was a reality that he had borne for years and talking about it would change nothing, and yet didn't the burden of it suddenly feel a little lighter, its sting a little less potent?

His phone rang but, without breaking their eye contact, he swiped a finger across the screen to reject the call and, before Rae could cajole any more confessions out of him, he moved on. 'Are you ready for dessert? Your favourite is on the menu—tiramisu.'

Just as he reached for the menu, his phone buzzed once again.

'*Mi scusi.*' With a quiet growl of annoyance, he snatched it up, intent on giving the caller an earache for disturbing him, not once but twice. But then he sighed as he listened to the voice on the other end of the line, hanging up with a promise to be at the office soon. 'I'm sorry, Rae. There's a crisis with a new deal we're working on and I need to go and deal with it in person or it could fall apart.'

He was aggravated, and not just because his prize deal had hit a snag, but because it meant cutting short his evening with Rae.

She smiled across at him. 'It's okay. Don't worry. I couldn't eat another bite anyway.'

Her words didn't dispel his niggle of guilt, or the feeling that he would prefer to stay with her, even though he didn't understand why he was feeling that sudden yearning for closeness with her.

'I'll sort the bill and walk you back to the palazzo.'

'You don't need to do that. You need to hurry. I can get myself home. It's not far.'

'You're not walking back alone. That's final,' he added when she opened her mouth to protest, the thought of her navigating the darkened streets alone sending trickles of fear seeping down his spine.

Throwing down a set of bills on the table, Domenico

took her hand, leading her from the restaurant and making their goodbyes. Only a few of the photographers who'd been documenting the arrivals of Venice's social elite remained, but they eagerly snapped yet more shots of Rae and Domenico as they exited onto the street.

The night was dark and quiet. Venice's streets and bridges and waterways were almost empty. The dark water was still, reflecting the glitter of the lights from the surrounding buildings. Domenico kept hold of her hand as they walked in silence, the gentle brushing of his thumb feeling the crazy skittering of her pulse, making him wonder if she was also sensing that new intimacy between them, if she was as aware of him as he was of her, every brush of her arm, the nudge of her hip.

'Am I allowed to ask what the crisis is?' Rae asked after a few minutes of quiet. 'Or is it top secret?' she teased and Domenico saw it as a sign that she was feeling it too, that whatever had shifted had done so for them both.

'It's fairly top secret, yes,' he said, slanting her a quick smile to keep the light mood in place because he didn't want to disturb that connection blooming between them. It was the closest he'd felt to another person in a long time and whilst that normally wouldn't have mattered to him, in that moment it did. 'But for you I'll make an exception. The Ricci Group is negotiating a big deal that will see us expand into operating a cruise line.'

Her eyes popped. 'Like Raphael always wanted?'

Domenico was surprised that she'd remembered. Surprised, and pleased. 'Yes.'

'Domenico, that's incredible. Congratulations.' Her

smile illuminated her whole face and Domenico's lungs squeezed. She was so beautiful, so much more than she knew, that it was actually painful. In the months that she'd been gone he'd encountered countless women, many of whom were eye-wateringly stunning, yet none had drawn from him a reaction that could compete with his response to Rae's smile.

'Thank you. It's been hard even getting to the negotiations. The company we want to partner with has a CEO who is notoriously guarded about who he deals with, but we've been making some good progress lately and I don't want anything to derail it.'

'Did Elena know about it?'

He gave a single nod of his dark head. 'She did. I told her a few weeks before she passed. When she took over Raphael's role as CEO she tried to realise that dream on a few occasions, but it never worked out.'

'I remember her telling me. I always got the sense that was a big regret of hers. She must have been incredibly touched that you were doing that.'

'*Sì*, she was.' The memory of that conversation, of all his conversations with Elena, rolled slowly through his mind, a million shards of memory causing a million throbs of pain.

He tried not to think about it too often—his default way of dealing with anything difficult—but he missed her. Missed her more than words could express. It was an ache that at times diminished but then always roared back into existence. At times he felt that, without her guiding presence, he had no sense of whether he was coming or going, no anchor tethering him to the earth.

It was an unpleasant snapshot of what his life would have been had Elena not stepped in and taken him in as a baby and it only sharpened his conviction that he had to succeed in this deal. He had to show Elena that she had been right to give him the chance in life that she had. Once more he needed to prove his worth.

'It must still be incredibly hard for you,' Rae said, watching his expression and reading everything in it, and abruptly he felt too exposed, too vulnerable, and he worked to shove those feelings back into the locker they'd sprung free from. Because he'd already told Rae too much, allowed her to glimpse too much of him. 'It's not been long since she passed. If you ever want to talk about it, about her, I'm here.'

As she made the offer, she watched him from those deep blue eyes and a potent emotional need stretched within him. A yearning to accept and tell her everything and deepen that tentative bond weaving itself around them like a magic spell. To reach out and grasp the comfort and connection she could provide and once more feel moored to something, someone. To feel that he had a place to call home, someone to call his family.

But they were dangerous yearnings that had to be cauterised. Ripped out, root and stem. Because chasing those feelings only led to heartache. That was a mistake he'd made already—he would not be foolish enough to do so again.

'I'm fine,' he said curtly, resuming a faster stride. If he said that enough times, believed it to be true, at some point it would start to be true, wouldn't it?

'Well, if at any time you change your mind, the invitation stands,' she said lightly, and was it his imagination or did Rae look a little deflated at his brusque dismissal? And why did that bother him?

They reached the palazzo. Lights burned in a few of the windows invitingly. Rae looked at the door and then back at him, a small smile on her lips.

'Thank you for walking me back. I hope you can fix whatever the problem with the deal is. Goodnight, Domenico.'

'Not so fast.' Domenico seized her hand as she tried to turn away. With a single step he moved closer to her, close enough to cause her breath to audibly hitch and her eyes to explode with colour. 'A man in love doesn't say goodbye to his wife for the night without a kiss.'

She swallowed and looked back at him nervously. 'There's nobody around, Domenico.'

There wasn't. But he didn't care. 'I'm not taking any chances,' he breathed, lowering his head towards hers.

It *had* been about making sure any lurking photographers or eavesdroppers had a show of them engaging physically. He was adamant about that, even though his lips had been tingling with anticipation of the moment their mouths would meet, but when the petal softness of her lips moulded to his and she responded with that gentle mewl of pleasing capitulation, his nerve-endings caught fire and the kiss became about something else entirely.

About coaxing more of that passion from her until she had no way of hiding from it. And revelling that in that heady, fevered pounding of his blood that she, and only she, could inspire.

Because this was something that Domenico understood and was happy to accept. Desire made complete sense to him, far more than those bewildering emotional yearnings that had surfaced with such strength only moments ago.

Banding his arms around her and drawing her tight against the wall of his body, he sought to squash those feelings into nothing, to incinerate them with the force of the heat blooming between their bodies, and with the passion of their kiss intensifying he could feel the confusion in his mind lessening, shrinking, until all made perfect sense again.

This was all that he wanted from Rae. Not her compassion, or comfort or understanding. He wanted the taste of her on his tongue, the feel of her arching and gasping beneath his hands. That was all permissible, the maximum he would allow himself to crave, to take.

And Rae was offering plenty of herself. Her hunger had overtaken her, her mouth moving against his with as much abandon and eagerness as his own, her chest grazing wantonly against his. She couldn't hide it. She sought everything that he did and as the flames of her desire licked against his own, they swirled into an even brighter, hotter, more treacherous fire.

Pressing her backwards into the wall of the palazzo, Domenico slowed the rhythm of their mouths, taking the kiss deeper as he slid his hands inside her jacket and around her body. Moving slowly, purposefully, they traced her waist, down over her hips and then around, exploring the toned peachiness of her bottom, the feel of her as exciting, as arousing, as dangerous as the taste.

He'd ignored and avoided this for too long, he realised with a burst of clarity. Too many nights he had lain awake, his sleep disturbed by his unfulfilled craving for the sweet connection with her body, and that had probably helped to cause the confusion in his mind, his body becoming overwrought with need and misinterpreting the signals being transmitted. But that was easily fixed.

'I think we may need to revisit the terms of our arrangement, *tesoro*,' he murmured against her lips, finding the power to momentarily break the kiss.

Rae's cheeks were flushed and she blinked a few times, a frantic look spreading across her face. 'What do you mean?'

'Us, Rae. *This*. We clearly both still want each other. We may as well take advantage of this time and enjoy ourselves.'

'No.' Rae shook her head, lightly at first but then with even more vehemence. 'No. Domenico. You're wrong. I don't…'

'Don't lie and tell me you don't feel it too, Rae,' he said huskily. 'I know your body, your kisses.' Even in that second, he could feel the hum of her blood, moving fast and hungry through her aroused body. 'I know you still desire me as I do you.'

An expression of panic shot through her eyes and she tried to put as much space as possible between their heated bodies. 'We're not having this conversation. We have an arrangement and the terms of it are fine. And now you should leave. You need to leave. There is a problem at your office and people waiting for you,' she reminded him sternly.

Domenico couldn't argue with that. The clock was ticking on his crisis. But if he didn't have to leave…

Using his finger, he angled her flushed and frantic face up to his. 'You may be able to run from this right now, but we will be talking about it again,' he promised, feeling the quiver skittering beneath her skin. 'What we have is too special to waste, Rae. So think about it… think about all the ways you know I can satisfy you. I know I will be.'

CHAPTER SEVEN

TAKING A BREAK from the sketch she had been focused on for the last forty minutes, Rae savoured a sip of her cool water and, leaning back in her seat in her favourite corner of the palazzo's courtyard, tilted her face towards the sun, enjoying the heat that kissed her cheeks. However, she had no sooner closed her eyes than Domenico loomed at the forefront of her mind, just as he had numerous times since the previous night, forcing her to snap her eyes open again to keep her thoughts from wandering too far off the beaten track.

The previous evening had been…unexpected. After the kissing incident at the gala she'd been nervous about being so close to him again and had expected that the night would be edged with the tautest kind of tension, an expectation that had seemed on point when Domenico had been quiet, almost distracted, when they'd set out from the palazzo. But then he'd amazed her by asking about Imogen and from then the conversation had unfolded with incredible ease. Admittedly, he had stayed true to form and redirected the conversation when he hadn't wanted to say any more on the topic of his birth mother, but it had surprised her how candid he'd been about his shattering experience as a young boy.

Having waited so long for answers about his past, any answers, it had been hard for Rae to not be greedy, to refrain from pushing for more information, but she knew how difficult it was to draw him out to speak about his memories and she hadn't wanted to scare him into shutting down entirely and so had let him change the subject, content that he had opened up at all.

Rae couldn't remember a time when he had been as open with her. As they'd walked home, he had even offered up details about The Ricci Group, but it was what he had revealed about himself and the past, which he carried like an albatross around his neck, that had stuck with Rae the most.

Learning that his mother had actually lived in Venice had astonished her, because she'd never been given any indication that there had been any contact between him and any of his immediate family members. Hearing that she had completely ignored his presence had rendered Rae speechless, heartbroken for Domenico that he'd been forced to face such callousness and livid with his mother at the same time. It was a good thing that she no longer lived in Venice because, now that she was privy to that information, Rae was certain she would not be able to cross paths with the woman and hold her tongue. Of course there could be circumstances that Rae wasn't aware of, but, regardless, Domenico had deserved better than that. He'd deserved some acknowledgement of his existence at the very least.

She'd watched the pain flicker like a dying ember

in his eyes as he'd recounted their encounter and the added admission that he'd crumpled the memory into something small and buried it away had torn at her heart whilst also explaining so much. If that was how he had handled any painful experiences over the years, he probably had a whole mental trunk stuffed with negative emotion that he never wanted to open again, hence why he'd resisted her every attempt to get him to open up. Perhaps he was afraid that once he let one thing loose, the rest would come tumbling out in an overwhelming tumult that would bury him.

It definitely cast his actions in a new light. In the past, Rae had taken his rebuffs personally, the rejection weighing heavy on her heart because she'd felt that he didn't want to share his secrets with *her*, that he didn't trust her enough to open himself up. But maybe his reluctance had always been more about his own fears. Maybe if she'd pressed harder, as she had last night, rather than backing off when he'd made it clear he wanted her to, they could have achieved that small breakthrough long ago.

Not that it mattered any more. The past was gone and their future extended only as far as the next six months, and, even if that deadline hadn't existed, Domenico still didn't possess the emotional openness that Rae wanted in the man she chose to share her life with. She wanted a partner whom she could talk to about anything, a partner who would be supportive and encouraging, who would meet her where she needed to be met, a partner who could share his feelings as easily as he shared his bed. That wasn't Domenico.

Their conversation last night had been good, and had reassured Rae that once she changed she could encourage change in those around her, but it certainly didn't mean that *he* had changed in any meaningful or permanent way.

Since a future together was not a viable option—and it absolutely wasn't—where was the sense in rekindling a sexual relationship that would only blur the lines of their arrangement? She knew with every rational breath she drew that it wasn't a good idea, yet...yet last night's kiss was playing over and over in her mind, like a song on repeat.

That hot, searing, purposeful claim his mouth had staked on hers had been like something from a dream. Tender but powerful. The full force of him had been contained in that encounter, making her feel as if the earth was shifting beneath her feet and she couldn't help but wonder if there was another man on the planet who could be capable of making her feel so much. Not that she was thinking about a relationship with anyone else. Her sole focus, for the moment, was on herself and creating the life she desired. When she'd left Venice, Rae had assumed that in time Domenico's mark on her would fade, but the more time she spent with him, the more confused she became because she realised how deeply her physical senses still belonged to him. Yearned for him.

It had taken far too long for her body to settle last night. *'Think about all the ways you know I can satisfy you,'* Domenico had said, and Rae had certainly done that. She hadn't been able to stop herself from thinking about it.

Those aching throbs low in her pelvis had continued to strike long after she'd showered and climbed into bed and, as sternly as she had ordered herself not to, Rae had yearned for Domenico to return and satisfy her in a way she hadn't ached for anything in a long time, even though she knew that was a path she must absolutely not go down.

But the tentative emotional connection that had threaded itself between them like a silken web had only made that physical yearning all the deeper. Because the time they'd spent together had highlighted how he could be a perfect partner. He'd listened so attentively to her concern over her sister and his response had been thoughtful and wise. After their conversation, the worry she'd been nursing had been somewhat allayed, his reassurance calming her.

She wasn't used to having someone to share her concerns with and it had dawned on Rae that perhaps that she hadn't always been the best at sharing her feelings or concerns either. Since losing her parents, she'd had to carry her worries alone. Her sisters had had more than enough to contend with in their grief and she'd never wanted to burden them more. Over time it had become her habit to keep things inside and to steady her fears herself.

So maybe if she had been better at sharing…matters would have unfolded differently. But there was no point in dwelling on that either. She couldn't alter the past and Rae knew that she had made the right choice in leaving. That was proven by the giant strides she'd made in building her own bridal collection in only a few short months. If she'd still been in Venice, still been a full-time Ricci wife, there was no way she would have had the time to outline her whole collection, source materials and design and produce nearly a dozen bridal and bridesmaids' gowns.

Her mother had made the choice to abandon her dreams of running her own catering company once she'd become a corporate wife. She had given over all of herself to the demands of Rae's father's busy professional life, and they'd enjoyed an enormously happy relationship, but where had it left her mother? She'd been devastated by her husband's untimely death and, without anything other than him to anchor her, had been swept away by a tide of grief and loneliness. Rae refused to follow her there. Refused to leave herself in a position for that to happen.

Whatever she was feeling for Domenico, she was unequivocal about that.

'I should have known I'd find you out here. It always was one of your favourite spots.'

Rae started, taken unawares by the low thrum of Domenico's voice, almost as if the strength of her thoughts had conjured him home, and as her eyes jumped to where the voice had come from, her heart leapt high in her chest.

'That's one thing that didn't change, I guess.' She smiled, her eyes rapidly sweeping over him, hungry to take all of him in all at once. In looking so close, Rae noticed how tired he looked. His dark eyes were ringed by even darker shadows, strain leeching out of his gaze. 'Were you working all night?' she asked with an undis- guised note of concern.

She knew he hadn't returned by the time she'd fallen asleep in the early hours because her ears had been straining to detect any sign of his return. Upon waking that morning, she'd wondered if he had returned with the dawn to change his clothes before returning directly to the office, but, judging by this suit, which, although immaculate, was the same one he'd been wearing last night, Rae guessed that hadn't been the case.

'Pretty much.' Domenico rubbed at his jaw, dusted with uncharacteristic dark stubble, and Rae had the sud- den urge to be close enough to feel it scrape against her skin.

'Did you manage to save the deal?'

'No. But I did get their CEO to agree to meet me in person to work out the problem.'

'Is he coming to Venice?'

'No. I'm going to him.' An alert sounded on his phone and he glanced at it, his fast fingers tapping out a reply in seconds. 'He has a luxury estate in Majorca and he's invited us to stay for the weekend.'

Having been ruminating on his absence over the weekend with a somewhat strange feeling spreading across her chest, it took Rae a second to process what he'd said.

'Us?' she repeated with an arch of her brow. Her pulse picked up as he began a slow stroll towards her.

'*Sì*. He invited me to bring my wife along and it would look odd if I showed up alone, don't you think?'

Her head started to spin as he drew closer, the scent of him hitting her first, and then the closeness of his body—forbidden, but welcome, oh, so welcome. Rae couldn't help but admire the outline of his chest through his shirt, the definition of hard muscle, coaxing her to touch. With superhuman effort, she dragged her eyes up to his, just in time to see the small smile playing around his lips.

'It also means we will have the opportunity to continue our conversation from last night.'

Rae knew that was her moment to tell him that conversation was closed. That it had started and ended last night. But, for some reason, her mouth wouldn't move and the words wouldn't form. And then his eyes were tracing over her face, pausing when they moved across her lips, and his fingertip was weaving a feather-light trail across her cheek and Rae was so close to forgetting her own name as she *ached* for him to lower his mouth to hers, to have the taste of him on her tongue.

'But later,' he drawled, leaving her lips still aching for that kiss as he dropped his hand. 'Right now, we both need to pack. We're wheels up in ninety minutes.'

Rae stilled, her heated thoughts draining away with the cold bite of reality.

Ninety minutes. She couldn't do that.

So far, there had been no conflict between Domenico and her growing business. She worked on her designs during the day when she was left to her own devices and Domenico had—unsurprisingly—never asked what she did with the hours she was alone. But she was going to have to tell him now.

He was already walking away and Rae took a deep, fortifying breath. 'I'm sorry. I can't leave in ninety minutes.'

He stopped, turning his head over his shoulder and a look of incredulity swept across his smooth features. 'You can't?'

'No.' Rae warred to keep her voice steady. 'I have an appointment.'

'Can't you cancel it? Rearrange it?' he asked too easily, too quickly, and it chafed at Rae in all the same ways and same places that it used to. Why did he always think her plans were of a lesser importance? That they could be *rearranged*? That she should jump whenever he clicked his fingers?

'No, I can't,' she said on a deep breath, making an effort to keep tight hold of her frustration, because an argument wasn't going to make this conversation any more palatable. 'I made a commitment and it would be rude and unprofessional of me to cancel at the last minute. Not to mention, the meeting is important to me.'

He stared down at her, his dark eyes rich with thought and his arms crossed over his broad chest as he considered her. 'What is this important meeting?' he demanded to know.

Rae mirrored his stance, folding her arms against her chest and meeting his assessing regard. 'It's a video call with a client.'

'A client?'

Rae nodded, acutely aware that this was a conversation she had shied away from having in the past—she shouldn't have, and wouldn't do so now. Her work was important to her. It was a priority, and Domenico would have to accept that, the same way she had always accepted his commitment to The Ricci Group.

'Yes. I've started designing a bridal collection.'

Picking up her sketchbook off the table, she handed it to him, holding her breath for him to accept it and start to flip through the pages. His eyes moved over each sketch, absorbing every detail with the same steady but indecipherable expression.

'Why didn't you mention this to me sooner?' he demanded, and there was something brusque about his tone that filled her with that old instinct to retreat.

But she wouldn't.

'You didn't ask, for one thing,' she pointed out sharply. 'But you're right, it was an error on my part to not tell you about it before now. Because this is very important to me and for the past number of months I've been working incredibly hard at it. My video call appointment this afternoon is with a bride who would like to talk to me about designing her wedding dress. She's seen others that I've been working on and is impressed.' Rae was aware that she was speaking to him in a way that she never had before, with unapologetic directness and clarity and as though she was his equal, and she sensed him regarding her in a new way in return. 'I understand the trip to Majorca is important, but so is this. So I'm sure there's a way to compromise. How about if I fly out later this evening to join you?'

'No,' Domenico decreed after a moment's thought. 'I'll push the flight back so we can leave after you've finished your appointment. Arriving a few hours later won't make that much of a difference.'

'Really?' Rae struggled to hide her surprise that he was being so...*amenable*. 'That's... Thank you.'

'You're welcome.' He nodded, before turning on his heel and walking away and Rae could only stare after him, unspeakably proud of herself and unspeakably shocked by Domenico.

Rae was occupied for most of the flight to Majorca, her head bent low over her sketchbook, her hands moving fast and furiously. Domenico watched her, curiosity smouldering in his gut. She'd come off her video call with a bounce in her step and a sparkle in her eyes that he immediately knew had been absent during her final weeks in Venice with him. He hadn't noticed that change in her at the time but, having taken a hard look back, he could see now that she had lost something of herself back then, and that was making him question exactly how great a factor her desire for a career had been in her decision to leave him all those months ago.

He had planned to spend the flight working, preparing for his meeting over the weekend, but instead he spent it deep in thought, being plagued by questions to which he didn't know the answers.

And he loathed those types of questions. He had enough of them haunting him already.

As Rae sat back and surveyed her work with a critical eye, her lips curling up with a small smile of satisfaction, Domenico saw his chance to indulge that curiosity.

'May I see?' he asked, moving to a seat opposite her.

After a small hesitation she nodded, turning her sketchbook towards him. He cast his gaze over the beautiful sketches, taking in the care, the attention to every detail and her unique flair that he'd noticed immediately in the designs she'd shown him back at the palazzo. He'd undertaken a quick internet search earlier—something he'd started to do so many times since she'd walked out on him, only to always stop himself because doing so would indicate an attachment and interest that he'd refused to acknowledge in his all-consuming anger—and had quickly noticed the growing awareness around her name. After seeing her work, Domenico could see that she deserved every word of praise being sent her way.

'You're making your bride two dresses?'

'Yes. One for the ceremony, another for the reception.'

He forced himself to listen, even though all he wanted to do was grab her and not let go until she'd given him the answers he craved. That burning need he'd repressed for the past weeks and months had escaped its confines and was spreading like wildfire through him.

'This is the ceremony dress. All of it will be Alençon lace: very luxurious, very romantic. It's also very expensive, but it shapes beautifully and is durable enough to accept the beading she wants.'

'It's beautiful, Rae. All of these designs are.' He raised his eyes to hers, his stomach tightening as he saw it again, that gleam of unbridled joy and fulfilment. Given that he had once been responsible for that happy sparkle in her eyes, that he had been the man she'd wanted to share her life with, he couldn't fathom why she hadn't shared any of this with him. 'I have to admit, I'm curious how this all came about,' he said, sweeping an elegant hand over the book and the designs and keeping his voice more steady than he felt.

Rae hesitated again, her slim throat moving nervously and the tip of her tongue darting out to moisten her lips. The innocent act had desire firing to every corner of his body even as his mind was focused on getting answers.

'Do you remember Nell Parker—I was in Venice for her wedding when we first met? I'd helped redesign a dress for her...' He manged a stiff nod, coiled tight with anticipation, sensing answers were on the horizon. 'Well, she runs her own investment firm and she was so impressed by my design that at the time she said that if I ever had an interest in striking out my own, she'd be interested in investing in me. I called her a few months ago to see if the offer still stood, and it did but, coincidentally, she'd been trying to reach me too because her sister was in the middle of her own wedding crisis. Her reception gown and bridesmaids' dresses hadn't turned out how she wanted and she remembered loving Nell's party dress and so wanted my help. So I helped. And then, after her wedding, more people wanted my details. So I'm taking commissions whilst building a collection to show Nell before we make any partnership official. I figure that if I already have a client base and I can prove that there's a demand for my designs then I'll seem like an even better prospect for investment.'

'That's smart,' he commented, impressed at the savviness with which she was approaching the venture. 'Obviously, I knew you worked as a consultant at the bridal boutique back in London, but I wasn't aware that you wanted to design your own collection or have your own brand. You never told me,' he said, failing to keep the small quiver of accusation from his tone.

'I know.' Rae's eyes briefly met his and she swallowed nervously. 'The truth is I was afraid to. Afraid that a wife with career ambitions wasn't what you wanted.'

'You thought I wouldn't be supportive of you wanting a career?' he demanded, searching for clarification of what she hadn't said.

'Not really, no,' she admitted, and an uncomfortable heat swarmed into Rae's cheeks as she spoke that truth into the taut air between them.

Domenico's mouth dropped open. He was unable to understand what foundation she had to base that unflattering assumption on, because he had always been incredibly supportive of her. He'd...

But the silence in his head as he tried to root out examples to prove his point was deafening and as vehemently as he wanted to argue his case, he knew he could not.

'You liked our life the way that it was, Domenico, with me being available to you most of the time,' she expanded into the silence. 'I didn't think you would be eager to see that change, not when you had made it very clear early on in our relationship that you liked having me by your side and with you as much as possible.'

'And that's something I should apologise for?' he demanded, more agitated than he wanted to be, but the failings he'd just been awakened to were weighing heavily on his chest and her words had ripped through him like bullets. Because everything she said was right. He had wanted it to be exactly as she described. The pleasure and security of having her always by his side, always within reaching distance. Against all the odds, he had found someone he cared for enough to let into his life, someone who'd cared for him in return, who had wanted him to be her present and her future, and he'd wanted to hold on to her as tight as he could. It had never occurred to him that'd he'd been holding on too tight. 'You were my wife, Rae. Of course I wanted us to be together all the time. That was the point of us getting married, wasn't it?'

'Yes.' Her blue eyes glittered, brimming with too many emotions for him to discern any of them. 'But I didn't realise that marrying you would mean surrendering all of myself to you. I thought it would be a partnership.'

'It was a partnership,' he insisted, even though he was starting to see that there had been some inequalities, for which he bore a heavy responsibility.

'Perhaps from where you stood. But for me... I was so busy living *your* life with you, I didn't have any time to live my own and I needed that,' she said, looking very close to tears. He had realised it already, but those shining pools of emotion in her eyes made it clear that this had been no trivial matter. He only wished he better understood *why*. 'I needed to have a life of my own, Domenico.'

Looking across at her, Domenico's throat felt too tight and too dry, his heart squeezing as if being tortured by invisible hands. He considered himself an astute reader of people, but he'd never seen, or even suspected, that Rae felt that way and he hated that he'd been so blind. So ignorant. That he'd failed her as a husband.

Failure had never been an option for him, not in any area of his life. Even as a young boy, long before he had learned the truth of his birth, he'd always known he was incredibly fortunate to have been taken in by Elena and he'd always felt the weight of that fortune, felt the need to prove himself, to make sure she had no reason to turn her back on him. So he'd made sure he was always as close to perfect as possible. He'd mastered every task, every skill, studying long into the night to overcome his learning difficulties and excel at academics, understanding all there was to know about the workings of The Ricci Group.

Upon marrying Rae, he had adopted the same mindset. Be the best man and husband possible. To him, that had meant formalising their relationship as soon as possible, claiming her as his wife in all the traditional ways and taking care of her financially, showering her with luxury.

Only that hadn't been enough, because it hadn't been right. That hadn't been what she wanted or needed from him and he hadn't known that because he hadn't taken the time to ask, to understand.

'I never knew you were unhappy with how things were,' he forced out, unable to keep the tremor from his voice as feelings twisted his insides.

Rae's blue eyes bored into his. 'You never asked.'

'And you never told me,' he shot back, suddenly as annoyed with her as he was with himself. Because he might have been ignorant, but she had been silent. She had known and hadn't given him a chance to fix the issue and make it better. 'If you ever needed or wanted anything, Rae, you only had to talk to me, to tell me.'

Didn't she know that he had only ever wanted to make her happy? To give her everything he possibly could. To make up for all the pain she'd had to endure in losing her parents at such a young age and selflessly and unwaveringly taking on the care of her two younger, grief-ridden sisters. Hadn't he shown how flexible he would be that afternoon, changing their flight arrangements so as not to disrupt her work engagement?

She gave a short laugh. 'Except every time I tried to talk to you about *anything*, you shut it down. You shut *me* down,' she exploded emotionally. 'In the end, there was no point in trying any more, because I knew what would happen. You'd walk away or you'd kiss me and we'd end up in bed and we'd never go back to the conversation. And if we couldn't talk about things, what kind of marriage did we really have?' She paused on a sad and heavy sigh, squeezing her eyes shut as though she had the power to blot out the painful memories. 'In the end, it was easier to leave.'

Domenico stared back at her, adrenaline pulsing through his veins and thoughts spinning through his mind, but unable to find any words in response. Unable to find his voice. Because Rae was holding up a mirror and forcing him to take a hard look at his own behaviour, and what he saw he didn't like at all. He'd made her feel shut out and disregarded and unsupported, and she had left because of that.

Because of him.

The realisation boomed in his mind like a roll of
thunder, and on its heels frustration and guilt and self-
recrimination tore through him, that conflagration of
emotions so strong he felt as if they might burn him
alive.

CHAPTER EIGHT

DOMENICO BARELY SAID ten words to Rae for the rest of the journey.

He was silent as they disembarked the plane and settled into the waiting car, a silence that continued as they made the journey from the airport to the villa on the northern tip of the island. When the car rolled through the large gates marking the entrance to the private and luxurious estate and Rae turned to him to comment on that striking first impression, she received only a distracted murmur in response and their arrival at their villa—a sprawling two-storeyed, white-and-glass-walled modern construction with access to a private slice of beach—elicited little more from him.

Now she was moving through the mundane motions of unpacking her case in a desperate effort to banish the edginess jangling in her body and mind. But, no matter what she did, she still felt...*rattled*.

They'd finally had the conversation that Rae had run away to avoid having and it had been as uncomfortable and unsettling as she had feared it would be, forcing her to speak her truth and exposing all the fissures and fault lines than had run through their relationship. And now the matter of their marriage, which had felt like a closed book, felt very much alive and present again, with all those truths colouring the air and mood between them.

She hadn't thought it would be easy, but she also hadn't been truly ready for how hard it would be either. For that level of honesty and frankness between them, or the way they had put their marriage under a microscope for inspection and dissection. It was brand-new territory for them and to Rae it was terrifying, having to pry herself apart to get to the heart of the matter. She'd always considered herself quite an open person, but once again she was realising just how inept she had been, and possibly still was, at divulging her innermost thoughts and feelings. The discomfort churning in her stomach at that realisation about herself was substantial, because she'd harboured so much frustration and resentment towards Domenico for his unwillingness to let her in emotionally, but she was guilty of the same failing. She hadn't let him know her feelings, her scars and insecurities, had she? And, rather than divulge them to him, she had packed her bags and fled!

She hadn't even been as honest as she could have been—or should have been—in that conversation. Yes, she had bared more of herself than she had in the past, but she had not told him *everything*. She had not opened up about her mother and how affected she'd been by her husband's death, the deep depression she'd sunk into and never emerged from. And until Domenico knew that part of Rae's story, how could any of her actions make sense to him?

But baring that to him would require letting him in

even further to her heart and soul, a prospect that was heart-stoppingly frightening. Because then he would know her in a way that no one else did. He would know all of her, even the broken places deep inside her.

Her anxiety levels spiking at the thought of generating such intimacy with him, Rae rose from the edge of the bed and wandered out onto the balcony, grateful for the gentle caress of the cool evening air against her too warm skin. Resting her arms atop the slim ledge, she closed her eyes, pleading with her body to settle down, but the peace was disturbed by the slap and splash of water.

Peering downwards towards the infinity pool, she saw Domenico slicing through the water, the span of his arms large and strong, his broad body a flash of bronzed gold in the clear water. Her body coiled, tensing with the rush of heated feeling, and Rae looked harder, wanting to see more of him, her heart kicking in her chest and, just like that, the memory of last night, of that solid body pressed up against hers, whipped through her mind, making her head whirl.

She imagined herself going down to him, quietly slipping off her clothes and joining him in the pool, letting the water carry her towards him until they were body to body, flesh against flesh. Until there was just the simplicity of desire, the complexity of all other emotions banished.

Alarmed by the force of the need pressing in on her, Rae hastily drew back into the shadows. That would be a very bad idea indeed. She wasn't there to relight anything and she didn't need to get in even deeper than she already was. What she needed was to remain detached enough to walk away intact at the end of the six months. So if Domenico was wounded and annoyed, maybe the wisest thing was to allow it, to let the issue wedge itself between them and prevent any further closeness.

But…her conscience prompted.

But…didn't he deserve a full explanation? Wasn't it only fair to both of them to clear the air completely, so that they could put the past to bed and move on? Based on the mess they were currently in, hiding her thoughts and feelings hadn't worked out well in the past, and as long as she concealed that piece of her past from him, wouldn't she remain uneasy, troubled by her cowardice?

She'd agreed to the arrangement to prove that she had changed and grown as a person, and perhaps learning to be more comfortable speaking her emotional truth was part of that journey too. And she could hardly continue to bemoan Domenico's emotional secrecy if she wasn't willing to be unreservedly honest herself. Even if the thought of letting him know her that deeply, that intimately, was absolutely terrifying…

But there was no time like the present, she decided and, without giving it another moment's thought, she turned and started down the steps towards the pool.

The swim had been a good idea.

Powering through length after length of the infinity pool had eased the spinning of Domenico's mind, and helped him to wrestle the demons and insecurities back into the box they'd sprung free from following all of Rae's startling revelations.

As he rested his arms against the edge and admired the glorious view as the sun disappeared into the horizon and painted the sky with streaks of sunset pink and red and wisps of fiery orange, he felt much calmer and in far better control of himself, which he needed to be. The outcome of the deal with Lorca was resting on the success of the weekend. There was too much at stake for him to be undone by his emotions.

And yet it was not the all-important deal that his mind chose to focus on as he relished those moments of the evening quiet. It was Rae. And their marriage. And all the ways he had screwed up.

He was a man capable of admitting to his mistakes. Elena had instilled in him the virtues of accountability and when he was wrong he could acknowledge it. And he'd been wrong in his marriage to Rae, neglecting her emotionally.

Every complaint she'd sent his way had been deserved. She'd had no reason to believe that he would support her aspirations because he'd never shown any interest in that part of her life. Never had he enquired about her dreams or ambitions for the future. He'd known she'd loved her job in London, but not once had he encouraged her to find a similar role in Venice.

Why hadn't he? Because he hadn't thought to. Hadn't cared to.

He mentally cursed himself again, the newfound awareness ravaging him in the same way it had on the plane. Over and over again he'd mulishly argued that there'd been nothing wrong in their marriage and that

Rae had had no good reason to walk out on him, but the opposite was true. He had let her down in so many ways.

And he hadn't even realised that it was happening.

Hearing the patter of footsteps behind him, Domenico turned to look over his shoulder, his body tightening as his eyes landed on Rae walking around the edge of the pool. Her feet were bare, her hair was hanging down in loose waves and she wore the same white trousers and blue blouse that she'd travelled in. Heat raced through his veins as his eyes followed her. There was no point ordering himself to look away. He knew he wouldn't. Couldn't.

There was no way to escape his feelings for her. No matter what had happened in the past, he wanted her with a heat that could not be quelled or contained.

'Can we talk?' she asked, coming to a stop, and as he read the solemn set of her expression, his mood darkened momentarily.

'Haven't we dredged up enough of the past for one day, Rae?'

'It will only take a few seconds,' she responded, shooting him a look that signalled she would not be deterred and he knew that, fired by her new grit and determination, she would not be.

'Bene.' He placed his hands on the side of the pool and levered himself out, completely naked. He reached for his towel, wrapping it around his waist before turning back to Rae. But as he did so he caught her widening stare, full of wonder and hunger.

She wiped her expression clear and started to speak. 'I want to apologise to you. Since our conversation, I've not been able to stop thinking about everything that happened between us and I realised it was wrong of me to run away. It was cowardly and unfair. I should have talked to you, told you what I was feeling and thinking. However hard it seemed to be, I should have tried, at the very least. And I'm truly sorry that I didn't, and that it's taken me this long to apologise.'

'Thank you for saying that,' he said, his voice quiet as he absorbed the depth of emotion in her expression. But she was not the only one who had been engaged in some serious self-reflection and although he could sense there was more she had to say, he couldn't allow her to go a second longer feeling that she bore sole responsibility for the demise of their relationship, so he pressed on. 'But what you said about me on the plane…you weren't wrong. I did like having you by my side all the time and I wouldn't have wanted that to change.' He lifted his shoulders, trying to loosen his thoughts. 'I wasn't trying to restrict your life, Rae, or you. I didn't even think of it in those terms. I was only thinking that I didn't want to lose that sense of complete belonging that I had with you. Because I'd never had that feeling before. I'd never felt like I belonged anywhere or to anyone.' His mouth was dry with the effort of speaking those words, those feelings dragged from the closed-off heart of him.

But Rae had every right to know why he had behaved as he had, where his ignorance and incompetence had stemmed from. He *wanted* her to understand. He wanted to understand it too and by the way she was hanging on his every word, whatever she had been on the verge of saying forgotten, he knew she was just as eager for that explanation.

'Did you feel that way because of the situation with your biological parents? Because you weren't raised by them?' she asked tentatively, as if she were tiptoeing across a minefield, expecting an explosion at any second.

Was that really what he'd done to her? Made her think she couldn't ask him anything? Fresh recrimination speared him, sharp and deep.

His nod was quick, an admission he didn't want to make and yet knew he had to. He had to start making amends, undoing these patterns that he hadn't known existed but that had proved so destructive. Moving to one of the nearby loungers, he sat down, gesturing for Rae to do the same.

'I was only a few days old when my mother abandoned me. She left me on the doorstep of Palazzo Ricci for someone inside to find.' He heard Rae's shocked intake of breath, but carried on. If he looked at her, if he paused, he wasn't sure he'd be able to continue. The only way for him to get through this was to keep going. 'She hadn't given me a name. She hadn't registered my birth. On my birth certificate it just says *genitori ignoti*—parents unknown. I've never been able to find out who my father is and my mother, whose identity I obviously did know, didn't want any connection with me.' His heart burned uncomfortably with that admission. 'I had no sense of belonging to anything, or anyone, not the way most children do. I had Elena and all the love she gave, and for that I was lucky, but she wasn't my mother and I always knew that. I was always aware that I didn't belong to her in that traditional sense and other children were very good at making me even more aware of that.'

And the steps that could have been taken to instil him with that security and sense of belonging had never been actioned. He didn't hold that against Elena. She had given him so much, but that additional piece of paper would have offered him a lot too. Instead, he'd grown up always feeling unsure—denied and rejected by one family and always fearful that it could happen again because there was nothing official, nothing legal, binding him to Elena. The first time he'd felt completely secure in a relationship, he realised with a jolt, was when he'd met Rae.

She'd been so open and giving of herself, so wholehearted in her acceptance of him. He'd liked how everything she felt was written across her face, how her arms opened to him whenever he walked in the room, the eagerness of her kisses. He'd felt so certain of her love for him.

Maybe that had been the driving force behind his whirlwind proposal, why he'd felt that loosening of feeling around her, why he'd been so impatient to marry her. Because all along he'd been clinging to that rarefied feeling, having finally found what he'd spent his whole life hungering for. Love and acceptance and belonging. And he'd wanted it legal and binding before it could be taken away.

Rae was quiet, absorbing the overwhelming weight of all that he had shared as the darkness swelled around them, cocooning them in its mystical embrace. When she did open her mouth to speak, he was expecting sympathy and platitudes but she just smiled sadly across at him.

'If only we could have found our way to talking like this four months ago,' she said wistfully.

'Would it have made a difference?' Domenico asked, unsure why he was asking the question or if he really wanted to hear the answer.

Her lips twisted as she thought about it. 'I'm not sure. Maybe. Knowing that we had the ability to talk things through would have helped me to feel a lot surer about our relationship. That we could have the big conversations. And I like talking to you, hearing the sound of your voice.'

'You didn't like the way we spent the time not talking?'

Her burst of laughter was quick and genuine. 'I had no problem with that. The physical side of our marriage was never in question. That was always incredible.' Her eyes glowed with the memory and her accompanying smile was almost shy. 'It's probably why I let myself be distracted by it so many times, because it was so good. Because it was in those moments, lying in your arms, that I felt closest to you. But it shouldn't have been a substitute. It wasn't. It's not.'

He heaved out a sigh, feeling the reproach. 'I'm not a man who wears his heart on his sleeve, Rae. I never pretended to be.'

'I know you didn't. But I thought that after we were married you would lower those walls a little, show me some more of yourself. That you would talk to me about…anything. Everything. The way my parents did.' She hugged her arms around herself, smiling nostalgically as she thought of them the way she always did, with that mix of happiness and hurt. 'I used to listen to them after we'd gone to bed. In the summer I'd leave my windows open and they'd be outside and I'd drift off to sleep to the sound of their voices. My mum talking about whatever naughty thing Maggie had done that day, my dad telling her about work. I stupidly assumed all marriages would be like that, and that ours would be too,' she confessed and Domenico felt a twist in his chest that he'd ruined such a simple dream. 'I didn't understand the amount of work that went into getting to that place. And when you wouldn't talk to me, I saw it as a rejection of me. That you didn't want to talk about things with me, you didn't trust me. Sometimes I even wondered why you'd married me, if you'd started to regret it. That's why it hurt so much.'

'Rae, no,' he assured her hurriedly before the words had even finished leaving her lips. 'That couldn't be further from the truth. I trusted you more than I ever trusted anyone. Before you, I had never considered letting anyone so deeply into my life. I just…'

The sledgehammer of guilt cut off his words as he was confronted by another of his inadequacies. The way he had shut her out.

He'd never liked talking about the past because experience had taught him that no good ever came from raking up dirt and searching for skeletons. And delving into emotional waters held no appeal, because his were cold and dark and he was scared of drowning in them.

He'd blocked those conversations to protect himself, but he'd failed to consider how that would be perceived by Rae. How it would make her feel. How it would affect the rest of their relationship. But he could see it now. See the walls he'd erected, the doors he'd sealed shut, locking her out completely. Domenico knew how that felt, and that he had forced her to feel that same dismissal was agonising.

'I never meant to shut you out, Rae. To shut down our conversations. But I'm not sure that I knew how to let you in either,' he admitted with a wince of discomfort at such profound self-analysis. 'When things have been hard, I think the way I've always dealt with them is by compressing my emotions into something small and manageable and locking them away. They're not easy doors to unlock.'

'I think I've started to understand that about you already. And the things you've told me… I understand why you would want to bury them, keep them out of sight and out of mind.' She reached out to him, just a small touch of her fingertips against his bare knee, but he felt it everywhere. 'You didn't deserve to be left like that, to be burdened with those feelings. And you didn't deserve to be left the way I left you either. If I caused you more pain, I'm sorry. But I appreciate everything you've chosen to tell me. I know it's not easy for you.'

It wasn't. It was like drawing poison from a wound, but if opening up earned him that soft and loving glow in her eyes, he'd gladly tell her more. Anything, to keep her staring at him in that way.

'I'm sorry I let you down so badly.'

'We let each other down,' she said on a sigh and, as she looked across at him, Domenico could see a tempest of emotion swirling in her eyes, threatening at any second to spill over. She chewed at the inside of her lip, deliberating about something uneasily, hovering on the edge of speaking, of telling him something he sensed was important to her, but then she just shook her head, shaking the storm from her gaze. 'We both made mistakes.'

He wanted to tell her that his mistakes were tearing him up inside, that he'd never wanted to lose her, that if he could go back and do it all over again, he would in a heartbeat. But he didn't know how to get those words out, didn't know if it would be wise to speak them aloud, so he just reached out, curling a hand around her cheek and drawing her face close to his. He touched his mouth to hers softly, a kiss that said everything he wanted to say but couldn't. And then he let her go.

'Did you think there was someone watching us?'

'No,' he said with a smile. 'That kiss was just because I wanted to kiss you.'

Her breathing changed, quickened. Heat exploded in her eyes, as if he'd set something loose inside of her, and then she asked, 'And if I wanted to kiss you back?'

'I wouldn't stop you.'

He wouldn't be able to stop himself. He couldn't tear his eyes from her, his hands were burning to feel her skin beneath his.

Rae moved at the same time he did, reaching out with as much urgency, so when their bodies collided and their lips fused together it was like a giant starburst, with pops of colour exploding behind his eyes and rivers of feeling pouring down his body as if a dam had broken.

CHAPTER NINE

THE PASSIONATE CLAIM Domenico was staking on her lips was making Rae's body tremble and her blood sing with delight. She'd missed this, she thought in the tiny part of her brain that was still capable of thought. Missed the masterly glide of his firm lips against hers, missed the bite of his hands into her tender flesh, and the feel of every line and contour of him pressed up against her. The moment was almost too overwhelming, every sensation fighting for dominance, and she couldn't decide which to revel in first…the imprint of his firm, masculine form or the deepening probe of his tongue, turning the desire already racing through her into a swirling inferno that was so potent it had the power to burn her from the inside out.

The last place that she had expected to end the evening was in Domenico's arms. And yet it felt right. More than right. *Necessary.* As he'd opened up, Rae had felt herself falling deeper and deeper into him, her body yearning to reach out to his and envelop him in her comfort. He had been so open and honest and she had wanted to be too, but when the moment for her transparency had arrived, Rae hadn't been able to do it. She had kept her secret locked inside, and chosen not to feel bad about doing so because, whatever it was between her and Domenico, it wasn't substantial enough to require the baring of her heart and soul. Their relationship was neither real nor lasting.

But then he abandoned the glorious assault on her mouth and feasted instead on the super-sensitive skin of her neck. As he scraped his teeth against the very spot he had just finished sucking on, Rae curled her fingers into his hair and snatched in a desperate lungful of cool air, needing that burst of oxygen because she was already drowning.

In him.

The feeling that speared through her seemed to be a direct and defiant repudiation to her stance that their relationship wasn't real. With every swipe of his mouth and every sweep of his hands Domenico was taking her over, inch by inch, kiss by kiss, and as he did, the parts of Rae's world that had felt out of sync for reasons she hadn't been able to identify began to shift back into perfect alignment.

She had spent so much time and energy trying to convince herself that she was okay without Domenico, that there was nothing missing from her life, but in that moment, with the imprint of his hands all over her and the sharp masculine scent of him surrounding her, she had no choice but to abandon that lie. Because she was coming alive again under the possessive pressure of his fingers against her skin and the hungry scrape of his mouth, and something very *real* was unfurling within her, something with a potent, glittering, unfamiliar power.

His hands moved to her blouse, reaching for the buttons, and as he did, he drew back enough so that he could stare at her. The look in his eyes was so hungry and yet so tender that Rae suddenly found it harder and harder to breathe. Because whilst they had done this many, *many* times before, for some reason it felt like the first time again. There was the remembered thrill and anticipation, but every other feeling spinning up inside her was so new, so profound and piercing, that she felt, just for a second, so wildly overwhelmed.

She could feel the thuds of her heart in her throat and they only grew heavier as he pushed the fabric of her blouse open and gazed down at her, hunger darkening the glow of his already dark eyes, turning them molten.

'You're so beautiful, Rae,' he breathed, and the sentiment seemed infused with so much loving and open feeling that tears hit the backs of her eyes.

'So are you.' Lifting her hand, she stroked it across his face, caressing the strong jawline and noble chin, brushing a finger across his full lips. It was a face she knew well, a face she would be able to find even in the dark, but now, as she looked into his eyes, for the first time she felt as if she could see into him, into his heart and soul, and she trembled. Because she had always wanted all of him, and now he was giving her exactly that. Only there was danger in that as much as delight, because the connection crackling between them was now all the more poignant and powerful. And it would be so much harder to extract herself from.

However, there was no question in her mind about turning back now. She wanted this connection with him. She was craving it. She needed it.

'Take me inside, Domenico,' she commanded in a whisper, knowing they needed privacy for all that she wanted to unfold.

He inhaled a sharp breath as though he hadn't dared imagine he'd hear those words, and then raised himself to his feet and carried her with him, her legs curled around his waist, her body cradled in his strong arms.

They didn't look away from each other, but neither of them spoke. To do so would have interrupted the feeling flowing unspoken between them and, finding his way inside, Domenico set her down on the nearest flat surface.

The light in the room was dim, casting a dusky glow, and his mouth wasted no time in reuniting with hers, his lips asking questions that she answered with her own. Their kisses deepened, the effect sinking deep within her, making the honeyed river of lust flow with more speed, more ease. When he drew back to take a breath his chest moved up and down in an uneven rhythm and Rae's heart and pulse were just as restless, running riot beneath her skin.

Reaching out, she traced her hands over his chest, revelling in the smoothness of his skin, the unbeliev-able strength of his body. His was the first, and only, male body she had ever touched and tasted and explored, and although she had no comparison, she knew there could be none. Domenico had no equal, and definitely no superior. It was not a theory she'd been in any rush to test, but she knew without question that no one would be capable of making her feel all that he did. Lightning, after all, did not strike twice.

She kissed a pathway across his chest, her lips settling over his heart—the heart that had been twisted and torn by the cruel actions of others. He thought he'd never belonged, but he belonged with her. In that room, in that moment, there was nowhere else on earth he should be and Rae was determined to use all the power of her body to show him that.

Hands gliding downwards across the corded muscle of his stomach, she loosened the tie on the towel and let it fall away, a breath quivering from her mouth as his arousal jutted into the space between them. Her chest hitched, her mouth running dry as her blood ran even hotter. She'd forgotten what a magnificent sight he was and the jagged, restless feeling cut through her again, and she could almost *feel* how good it would be to have him inside her once more, filling her, completing her. Owning her.

Watching her breathless reaction, impatience fired in Domenico's eyes and he reached for her clothes, sliding the blouse from her body, pulling the trousers down her legs and tossing them over his shoulder, and then he moved into the space between her thighs, running his sultry gaze down her body.

Lowering his head, he pressed a line of kisses down her throat and along the cup of the bra. Her reaction was instant, her flesh swelling against his mouth, her nipples tightening.

'Rae…' he groaned against her skin. 'I want to run

my mouth all over you, but I don't think I can wait to be inside of you.'

'So don't wait,' she urged, pressing herself into him, as desperate as he was to complete their joining.

With a single move, he positioned himself at her entrance and then, eyes locked with hers, he pressed powerfully into her, her body accepting every inch of the sweet penetration. He filled her completely and Rae gasped, not just with the joy of his possession but because of how different it felt. Rawer, deeper, more…just *more*. Her breaths crashed from her mouth, the moment feeling too big, too powerful, too moving. But then all she could feel was the exquisite familiarity of Domenico stroking inside her, tenderly but firmly propelling her towards her orgasm with the powerful thrusts of his body.

She clung to him, tilting her mouth up to receive his kiss, and he obliged, touching his lips to her mouth, her earlobe, her jaw, her neck, his breath like fire. His hands clasped her butt, urgency in his fingertips and his rhythm changed, the drive of his body becoming more powerful and possessive, and he surged deeper inside her, deeper than ever before, pressing her back to accommodate that exploration. With every move of his body, he obliterated her defences, taking more of her for himself, and the connection was electrifying. The beginning and the end. Everything that Rae had ever needed and felt like she would ever need.

He held on to her tighter, hitching her leg higher up his waist, and that was when she started to feel it, the onset of that wild, unstoppable ecstasy spiralling up through her body, consuming all of her with flagrant ease, and

Rae clung even more pleadingly to Domenico's shoulders, her mouth biting into his skin.

His own release was beckoning. Rae could feel him resisting, wanting them to hit their explosion point together, and seconds later they did exactly that. She broke apart with a cry of unadulterated delight a moment before he gave his own shout of release and, although they had made love a thousand times, the eruption was like nothing Rae had ever felt before and for an infinitesimal, heart-shaking moment she pulsed with the sense that nothing would ever be the same again.

CHAPTER TEN

RAE WAS HAVING the most exquisite dream.

Domenico's skilful mouth was marauding across her neck, swiping and sucking and nibbling. Where his lips and tongue touched, her skin tingled and sparks of glittering, explosive pleasure ignited by the blissful contact streaked along her veins, arrowing to the very centre of her body, where the most intense feeling was building. She arched her neck, offering him even better access, and speared her fingers into the thickness of his hair, purring at the back of her throat as his teeth and tongue played on the same spot, making her nerve-endings shiver and dance.

Then he began to tease more of her body. His hand slid languidly up her ribcage and curled around her breast. His fingers were warm and tender and her senses stirred even quicker at the intimate contact, straining beneath the touch, seeking more of it. His fingers brushed across her nipple, the large pad of his thumb circling the ultra-sensitised and begging point before flicking across it once, twice…a torturous three times. Her body arched and a gasp of wanton pleasure escaped from her parted lips, every inch of her now feeling alight and alive.

Enraptured by the caresses, Rae desperately wanted more of them, more of that heady, obliterating feeling he conjured within her. But, feeling the tug of consciousness, she squeezed her eyelids tighter together, wanting to stay in the dream as long as possible, not wanting to wake yet again to a darkened room and a cold, lonely bed. But the golden light of day was already infiltrating her gaze and as the pleasure of Domenico's touch built towards a crescendo her eyes flew open…and she realised it wasn't a dream at all.

Domenico's hands were skating across her body, his lips making her shiver as they trailed down her neck and towards her collarbone. Feeling was fizzing in every inch of her, her blood was humming and her body purring at his touch. Fragments of the previous night returned to her in bright flashes and Rae realised that it had happened. She hadn't only imagined it.

'*Buongiorno bellissima,*' Domenico murmured against her lips. They were the words he'd greeted her with every morning of their life together and Rae smiled, having never expected to hear them uttered again.

'I thought I was dreaming,' she whispered as he held her close. 'And I didn't want to wake up.'

He kissed her again, slow and long and deep, only pulling back to stare at her. 'Did you spend many nights dreaming of me?'

'Yes,' she admitted, tracing the sensual contours of his mouth with her finger.

During the day she'd never permitted him entry into her thoughts. During the dark secrecy of the night, however, when her consciousness had relaxed, she'd had no control over what—*who*—came into her thoughts. And Domenico always had. In the moment when it was said a person's deepest desires were revealed, he had always been hers. Rae had reassured herself that those mental slips were acceptable, normal even, and that with time her subconscious would relinquish its yearning for him.

But here she was, months later, in bed with him, and the feelings were as strong and imposing as ever. The shift of his hair-roughened leg against hers stirred detonations of delicious tingly feeling along her skin. The bulk of his body, so close, made her want him pressed up even closer. It made her question if her feelings for him would ever fade, but that was a worry she had no desire to dwell on in that moment. Worrying could wait until later. Much later.

'And what exactly was I doing in these dreams of yours?' His smile grew wider and wicked as a blush burned in her cheeks. 'Something like this, perhaps?'

Drawing her against him, Domenico buried his long fingers in the tumble of her hair and nuzzled his face in her neck and made her every wish come true as his naked body pressed up against hers. Rae moaned as his hard length moved against her, instantly suffusing her with the need to feel him inside her, filling her, claiming her. She pulled his head down, opening her mouth to his, excitement brewing within her as his tongue thrust between her lips in a dance that she knew only too well. A dance they had moved to several times during the night and, just like all those times before, the intimate slide of his body against hers transported her to heaven.

Later, she was resting, sated and sleepy, with her head

on his chest and his fingers stroking up and down her back in a lazy rhythm when Domenico's phone rang and he reached for it with his free hand. Rae already knew it would be Nico, Domenico's assistant, with his morning round-up.

'Morning, Nico,' Domenico greeted him, and Rae smiled as she felt the rumble of his rich voice vibrate deep within his chest. She'd missed that burr of his voice, missed the early part of the morning resting in his arms. It was in those moments that she had always felt most content, when her heart had felt beautifully full and her worries about their marriage had been diminished by the warmth and closeness of Domenico's presence.

However, her peacefulness was disturbed when Domenico vaulted into a sitting position, his body suddenly rigid.

Rae sat up too, clutching the sheet to her chest, concerned by the quick-fire chatter she could hear at the other end of the phone.

'Did you…? No… No, it's fine.' Domenico dashed a hand through his too long hair, shoving it back off his forehead and, based on that agitated motion and the stiffening line of his spine, Rae guessed that whatever it was that was going on wasn't fine at all, a theory confirmed by the heavy sigh he emitted upon disconnecting the call, followed by the torrent of blistering Italian.

Vaulting off the bed, he snatched at the first piece of clothing he found, anger infusing his every jerky movement as he pulled on the drawstring pants and started to pace backwards and forwards, hands planted on his lean hips. His Italian blood had always run red-hot with passion, and in recent days she'd seen him overwhelmed with feeling about his past, but Rae had never seen his temper heightened to such a degree and she was immediately wondering what had set it off.

'Domenico, what is it? What's happened?'

But he was already pacing away from her, brushing the flowing white curtain aside with an impatient hand and striding out onto the terrace, and Rae could only stare after him, bewildered.

Because in the space of thirty seconds the whole mood of the morning had changed and Rae was utterly unsure of what to do next. Not so long ago, she would have thought twice about rushing after him and querying his upset because she was so wary of being rebuffed. But things had changed a lot since then. She had changed, and the landscape between her and Domenico was shifting as well. The ground they had broken last night had been significant, and it was those moves that they had made to know each other better, *to trust each other*, which gave her the confidence to follow the instinct firing from her gut and follow him outside, where she hoped he would tell her what was bothering him.

The morning view was stunning, but all Domenico could focus on was the pressure pounding at his temples. The call from his assistant had delivered the worst news possible and with so much importance and emotion attached to the deal, and so much of his own self-worth tied to its success, his frustration was lodged so deeply he could barely think straight.

Hearing the gentle sound of footsteps on the tiles behind him, he emitted a sigh. 'Go away, Rae. Please.' The last thing he wanted was her witnessing the state he was in. He understood that he needed to be more open, and he was proud of the barriers he had been able to bring down last night, no matter how painful doing so had been, but this cut to the deepest and darkest of his fears and he was in no way ready to cast them into the light.

'Sorry. I can't do that,' she replied, her voice soft as she came to stand beside him. For a woman who bordered on being petite, only five-foot-four in height, he felt her presence immediately. 'Do you want to tell me what's going on?'

Absolutely not.

Turning his dark head towards her, Domenico was ready to repeat his earlier command, but as his gaze caught on her and he was hit between the eyes with the bright shine of her blue eyes and her long hair gleaming with the kiss of sunlight, he felt the knots around him loosen and, to his shock, heard himself start to speak.

'Lorca cancelled our sit-down today. His assistant phoned Nico ten minutes ago. She said that Lorca no longer has the time to meet me and that he sends his sincerest apologies, but still hopes to see us at his party this evening.'

Rae's brow furrowed slightly. 'You don't believe that?'

'He invited me out here to have that meeting, so why cancel it at the last minute?' he grated out, his voice frayed with aggravation. 'Unless he's stalling the deal on purpose.'

'Why would he do that?'

Domenico pushed his long fingers through his dark hair. 'I don't know. But every instinct I have is telling me that's what is going on.'

Rae's eyes rested on him, gentle and kind, and yet they seemed to burn him with their scrutiny. 'This deal with Lorca obviously means a lot to you. A lot more than any other deal I've ever seen you make,' she observed, and he could see her thoughts ticking over, trying so desperately to understand. She really was incredible. He'd neglected her emotionally, failed as a husband, but she was still standing at his side, trying to help him. Heal him. If it hadn't been clear to him before that moment, it suddenly was—he hadn't appreciated her enough in the past. Her strength, her kindness, her loyalty. He'd been so focused on his feelings, on the void in him that she had obliterated, he'd overlooked entirely the sensational woman he had been lucky enough to find. 'Is it because this was Raphael and Elena's dream? You're trying so hard to make it happen for them?'

'Yes, that's exactly it.'

'No, it's not,' Rae challenged gently, after a long moment studying him. 'You should know by now that I know when you're shutting me out, Domenico, when you're holding something back. What is it?'

In front of him, his hands curled into tight fists as he felt the truth bludgeoning its way to the surface from the depths where he had tried to bury it. 'I do want to do this for Elena and Raphael. I just also want it for myself too. To prove that I am deserving of the life that Elena gave me, that she was right to keep me, right to give me the position of her son and heir.'

He stared straight ahead, his eyes fixed on the neutrality of the sky, but all he could feel was the poison of that feeling slinking through his blood, making his heart race with the fear that it was the truth.

'Why would you need to prove that?' Rae asked on an aghast breath. 'Elena left you in charge of the company because she trusted you so much, and she gave you everything that she did because she wanted to, because she loved you.'

A muscle worked tightly in his jaw as the insecurity continued to needle at him 'She never made it official though, did she? She never formally adopted me, so there must have been some doubt in the back of her mind if I was worthy of all that she had to give.'

'Domenico, there could be a dozen reasons why Elena didn't adopt you, and none of them have anything to do with you not being good enough,' Rae argued. 'You are deserving. You are worthy. Your mother choosing to abandon you as a baby is a lot more damning of her character than of yours. You were just a baby, you did nothing wrong…'

'But maybe…'

'No maybe. You did nothing wrong. Look at me.'

Abandoning his forward stare, he turned his head.

Rae moved a step closer and pressed her hands to his chest, her eyes blazing with vehemence. 'You did nothing wrong,' she repeated, slower than the first time. 'There was nothing wrong with you. And even though your mother couldn't or didn't love you, Elena did and you have nothing to prove to her. But if you feel that you need to make this deal happen to believe that, then let's make this deal happen. Forget about the cancelled meeting. You'll speak with Lorca tonight at the party instead,' she said simply. 'All you need is a few minutes to talk through whatever is bothering him and sort it out. I've seen you close deals in less than fifteen minutes, Domenico, so you can do this, no problem. Don't let him cancelling today be a big thing. Take the opportunity to have a day to yourself, to take it easy. Enjoy the island.'

'I'm not someone who spends a lot of time taking it easy,' he muttered. 'You should know that.'

'I do know that. Which is all the more reason to do so now. You've been under a lot of pressure. You need some time to rest and destress so you're relaxed for tonight.'

She might be right, Domenico conceded with his eyes on the water below. He had been pushing himself harder than usual, partly because of this deal but also to avoid dwelling on his grief for Elena and his feelings about Rae's return. Maybe a day of leisurely pursuits would restore him to his usual pragmatic self and release some of the strain from his coiled body.

'What do you have in mind for this day of relaxation, then?' he asked her.

'Look at this beautiful island we're on. I'm sure we can come up with a few ideas.'

She smiled up at him, her eyes as blue as the waves rolling into the cove below them, and the tempo of his body shifted once more. Heat crackled in his veins and the simmering frustration melted away, only to be replaced with an entirely more pleasurable burn. They had shared a night of mind-blowing sex but, as satisfying as that reunion had been, Domenico was hungering to do it all over again.

He moved closer, succumbing to temptation and taking possession of her body with his hands. 'I actually already have a few ideas,' he shared as his fingers loosened the tie at her waist and delved beneath the silky fabric of her bright robe to meet the warm, soft skin beneath. 'And none of them involve you wearing clothes.'

'Wow.' Domenico went hard all over as Rae emerged from the bedroom. He'd thought she couldn't look any better than she had that afternoon when they'd spent a few hours on their private beach and she'd played in the waves in an emerald-green strapless bikini. However, in a pale gold sequinned wrap dress, with straps that curled up towards her neck and a neckline that dipped low enough to hint at the full swell of her breasts, she was a sight capable of setting him on fire. 'You look incredible.'

His eyes devoured every inch of her as his gaze swept from her head to her toes and then back again, a single look not enough. The dress showed off her figure to perfection—her toned legs, the sexy curve of her hips and slim waist, the globes of her breasts. The reaction of his body was immediate, his thoughts leaping ahead to when he could skim his hands across her body and peel away the material, sampling each piece of tender flesh as it was revealed.

'Is this one of your own designs?'

Colour bloomed in her cheeks. 'It is. An idea I was

experimenting with that didn't quite work out, but I loved it anyway. How could you tell?'

'I can see your touches in it.' Lightly, he touched the fabric between his fingers and then her, tilting her chin up to accept the graze of his lips. The taste of her as addictive as ever, he had to force himself to take a step back before he started to act on his fantasies and they never made it to the party.

'The car is outside. We should go. It would be poor form for us to be late.'

The journey to Lorca's home was brief, a short drive along the winding coastal roads with amazing views all around, the rocky outcrops on one side and the drop to the glittering blue waters on the other. It pleased Domenico that he was able to enjoy the view, his relaxed mood a drastic change from the tension that had been simmering in his blood for days, and perhaps weeks.

As much as he wished he could credit himself with the turnaround of his mood, it was Rae who had calmed him, reminding him of who he was and what he was capable of. It was her advice to take the day for himself, which had been the right thing to do, and it was her company that had made the day as fun and relaxing as it had been. It didn't surprise him but it did trouble him because, as his guard dropped, he was revealing more and more of himself to her. His deepest and darkest depths.

Rae had proved to be the balm he'd so desperately needed so he couldn't say he regretted sharing as much as he had, but he detested that she had witnessed him at his most vulnerable, when he was lost in the darkest reaches of his mind. It was not a place that he liked to go to, so to have shown it to her was…unsettling at the very least. He had never wanted anyone to know how damaged he was inside…but now she did. And if that valve on his emotions loosened any further then she would know almost everything, all the ugliness that he wanted to hide.

If their relationship had been secure, perhaps he could live with that, but right now she was his wife in name only. At least that was all she was supposed to be, but he knew a part of him had *wanted* to open up to her that morning. To let her in that way, to feel more of what he had felt the previous night. The peace that had come from sharing.

'You need her, Domenico,' Elena had insisted after Rae's departure, as she had tried to encourage him to go after her. *'You need her.'*

He'd denied it being true then, because how weak would a man have to be to admit to needing the woman who had turned her back on him? So, as happy as he was to have her by his side as they exited the car and walked up to Lorca's house, he was determined to re-sist it again now.

Because she *was* his wife in name only and in a mat-ter of a few months she would leave Venice and him. So there would be no more sharing of his emotional se-crets. The only intimacy they would share from now on would be physical.

CHAPTER ELEVEN

RAE GAZED OUT at the mesmerising view, staring at the spot where the indigo sky merged into the glimmering expanse of the sea. The stars were out in their thousands, the night air was balmy and so far it had been a wonderful night, following on from an idyllic day with Domenico.

Their seafood lunch at a waterside restaurant and afternoon enjoying their private beach had reminded her of the better days of their relationship, where everything had been so easy and carefree.

There had been a void in Rae's life before she'd met Domenico. In spite of her sisters and friends, her job at the bridal boutique and her dreams for the future, Rae had always felt as if something was missing. Something vital. She'd assumed it was the void left by losing her parents and the suddenness with which they'd dwindled from a family of five to one of three. But then she'd met Domenico and that void had evaporated. Suddenly everything had been dazzlingly, beautifully bright. She'd felt happy again, excited and hopeful in a way she hadn't in the longest time.

The same kind of happiness that was streaming

through her as she stood there, enjoying the evening. Had she been that happy after leaving him and returning to London? she caught herself wondering. Rae hadn't allowed herself to consider it at the time, but she knew it would be a lie to say she had been completely content. She'd made herself busy and forced herself to focus on the future, but without Domenico that chasm in her heart had opened again and she was only aware of it now because, after their day together, she felt it a little less keenly.

But she wasn't sure what she was supposed to do with that. As happy as Domenico made her, it could only be temporary. Because their time together had an expiration date, and once they hit it Rae would be returning to London.

Even though you have already thoroughly blurred the lines of your arrangement with him? And with each hour that passes you're only growing closer.

Rae's heart raced with her thoughts. They had grown closer, closer than they had ever been in the past. Even their intimacy had been different, charged by their emotional vulnerability with each other. There was only one matter that Rae had not yet shared with him—the truth about her mother's death—and that was proving to be a weighty burden. The guilt she felt about her continuing silence was immense because Domenico wasn't holding anything back. He had been raw and unguarded, answering any question she asked, and Rae felt that she was truly starting to know him, the real, beautiful, complicated man that he was.

At the outset she'd thought that getting answers to her

questions about his past would help her reach a place of closure, where she could walk away and leave him behind, but with all that she was learning her heart was opening up to him more than ever. And that was alarming to realise because one day their situation was going to end, and the more engaged her feelings became, the more likely it was that her heart would break into a hundred pieces when it did. Maybe that was another reason why she was clinging to her secret, because once Domenico knew everything she would belong to him in a way that was undeniable. And she wasn't ready for whatever it was between them to be anything more than what she had agreed to—a fake and temporary marriage.

'You're looking very thoughtful, Signora Ricci.' Drawn from her pensive moment, Rae looked up to see their host, Santiago Lorca, approaching at a leisurely pace. She had met him briefly when they had arrived and her first impressions had been of a warm and welcoming man.

'I'm just admiring these stunning views of yours,' she lied. 'The plot of land you have here is incredible.'

'It has been in my family for generations,' he shared, leaning back against the curved stone wall, 'apart from a brief period. When my father was a young man they went through some hard times and lost almost everything. It was a mission of mine to get it all back for him.'

'Was he here to see you achieve it?' Rae asked, hoping for a positive answer.

'He was, but he sadly didn't live long enough to enjoy it.'

'I'm sorry. That must have been very hard.'

'It was, but the upside is that I always feel connected to him here.' He paused, watching her with friendly eyes. 'Have you enjoyed the evening?'

'Very much.' In the ensuing silence, Rae's heart thudded. It wasn't her place to do so, and she had never before dreamt of meddling in Domenico's business dealings, but as she spied the opening to raise the topic of the deal, Rae knew she couldn't let it pass by. Although Domenico had recovered well from his troubled state that morning, and had so far charmed everyone they'd met that evening with his confident smile and magnetic charisma, she knew he was still singularly focused on getting the deal done. If there was any chance she could help, her heart was compelling her to try because the last thing she wanted was to see him mired in more despair. And now that she knew why it mattered so much to him… 'Although I noticed that you and Domenico haven't had the chance to talk yet.'

'Unfortunately not. Hosting duties are keeping me rather busy.'

'Is that the only reason?' Rae pressed, trembling within at her boldness. 'Domenico is worried that you're getting cold feet about the deal.'

'I do have some concerns,' Lorca admitted, much to her surprise. 'Given that history I just briefly touched upon, my company matters a great deal to me, and to the rest of my family. I am very conservative about if and who I enter into partnerships with. And your husband is in the middle of an emotional transition.'

'Because of the death of his aunt?' Rae queried.

'Precisely. And also, if you'll forgive me for being

so blunt, the rumours about your marriage.' With those words a hole slowly started to gnaw open in Rae's stomach. 'I'm not asking for an explanation; your personal life is private. But whilst Domenico always had a reputation for being pragmatic and unemotional, I worry that in having to contend with such issues he could become emotional. And emotional people are known to exercise poor judgement and take risks—the type of risks I don't want my company involved in.'

For a moment Rae couldn't speak. Her fingers had grown clammy around her champagne glass as all she could feel was the weight of the future of the deal on her shoulders. If she said the wrong thing in response, it could blow it to pieces. But if she could explain to him who Domenico really was, could she perhaps save it? And save Domenico from drowning in that fear of not being enough?

'Domenico would never be reckless with The Ricci Group,' she responded, the need to defend him rising in her like a tide. 'No matter what's going on in his personal life. The company belonged to the aunt who raised him, and before that her husband, and it means everything to him. Now that they are both gone, Domenico treasures it even more. He wants to make this deal for them, to fulfil a dream that they had. That's how you can be sure you can trust him, because he's just a son trying to make his parents' dream come true. And after what you just told me, surely you can understand that.'

'I can.' He nodded slowly before smiling across at her, the action sincere. 'I'm glad to have met you, Rae. You have given me an insight into your husband I didn't previously have.' He fixed his gaze on something over her shoulder. 'Your wife is delightful, Ricci.'

Turning her head over her shoulder, Rae's heart flipped to see Domenico sauntering closer. In his pale-coloured suit and open-necked shirt and with his hair gleaming in the starlit darkness, he looked almost too good to be true.

'She is. I'm a lucky man,' he agreed, sliding an arm that felt almost proprietorial around her waist.

'I don't want to interrupt your evening, but do you have a moment to talk now?' Lorca asked him. 'I have a fifteen-year-old Scotch I've been meaning to try. We can slip away for ten minutes.'

Domenico glanced down at her. 'Rae?'

'Go. I can amuse myself for a while.'

He pressed a feather-soft kiss to her lips before walking off in step with Lorca and Rae watched him go, happy that she had been able to help, yet uneasy about that happiness. Because there was only one reason that she would be so delighted for him, Rae recognised with a lump swelling in her throat. Because she still cared for him. More than she really should.

More than was safe, or smart.

More than she had actually realised when she'd agreed to their crazy charade.

But Domenico had always been quicksand. She only had to recall how quickly she had fallen for him in the first place. It had taken only hours and days for him to steal her heart. It really shouldn't surprise her he would be a stubborn presence to erase from it.

Feeling her pulse start to skip out of control with

her escalating worry, Rae attempted to comfort herself with the thought that it was different this time around, that *she* was incredibly different…but it was then that it hit her—because of those changes in her, *everything* between her and Domenico had become different too.

What they had now was not the same relationship that she had run away from. It was an entirely different beast, and that meant she was in entirely unchartered waters.

Later that evening, once they had returned to the villa, Rae was watching herself remove the delicate drop earrings from her ears in the mirror when she spied Domenico approaching in the reflection. Coming up behind her, one hand gently brushed her hair to one side before he touched his lips to the sensitive skin of her neck and feeling erupted along her skin.

'Thank you,' he breathed, his breath moving across her skin like a tender flame. 'For whatever it was that you said to Lorca.'

'All I told him was the type of man that you are,' Rae said, her eyes drawn into meeting his in the reflection by a magnetic pull that she couldn't fight.

'Whatever you said, it had some effect. We're meeting tomorrow morning to finalise the details of the contract.'

Happiness streamed through her again, making the nervous pit in her stomach grow wider, but she smiled back at him. 'Good. I'm happy for you.'

This time when he pressed a kiss to her neck it was open-mouthed. His tongue flickered against her hammering pulse point and it was like a flame being held to a tinderbox. Feeling exploded inside her. She wanted to hold back, to find some much-needed space to claw back the intensity of her growing feelings, but her body craved the opposite and as his lips trailed a line of fire up her neck and to her ear, and his hands started their slide of possession around her waist, Rae's eyes fluttered closed, her battle already lost. Her heart thundered with desire a hundred times stronger than anything she had ever felt before and all she wanted was to drown in the glorious feeling he conjured within her. To float in that space for ever.

She turned in his arms and he slowly lowered his head, but impatience ruled her actions and she rose to her tiptoes, speedily closing the distance between them and relishing that sinuous slide of his mouth against hers, need mounting frantically in her already, a hot and needy throb pounding in her molten core.

But whispers of warning continued to swirl around her mind. Where exactly would this leave her? She'd returned, amongst other reasons, to find some closure, but now all she was doing was drawing back closer and closer to Domenico, stripping back layer upon layer in a quest to know and understand him so much better. And the bond between them was intensifying, deepening... Would the boundaries of their original arrangement still be able to keep her safe? Or was she deluding herself, hiding behind an agreement that was no more stable than a sandcastle?

'Domenico, is this madness? Us doing this?' she breathed against his mouth, too needy for him to pull away but unable to quieten those thoughts.

'Possibly,' he murmured with a laugh. 'But it might

be madness not to do it too.' His body seemed to move closer to hers. 'As long as both of us are clear on the terms and time limits, I see no danger in it.'

Rae was almost certain she could see bright flashing red danger signs up ahead but they were dim, and with the sinuous slide of his hands taking her to a place where there were no negative feelings they seemed too far away to be of any immediate importance.

'Do you want me to stop?' he asked in between swipes of his lips over her neck.

The answer was on her lips before he'd even finished asking his question, rising from the very heart of her. 'No.'

Even if it was madness, it was a madness Rae wanted. Badly. With every breath she took and with every beat of her heart. Surely if she focused only on this physical need for him and not on the possibility of anything more significant, there could be no harm done.

Reaching for his mouth again, Rae responded to the gentle probe of his tongue by parting her lips and granting him entry to her mouth. She slid her tongue against his, hungry and needy and wanting. His fingers searched for the fastening on her dress and, with a deft move, undid it, gently sliding the straps from her shoulders and down her arms until the dress slid down her body to the floor in a whisper of sound. Domenico tore his mouth from hers to survey her body and his eyes burned with a shimmering flare as he took in the ivory lace lingerie set.

'I'm so glad I didn't know you were wearing this. I would never have been able to keep my hands off you,' he purred, his fingers lightly, teasingly skimming up and down her sides, touching and then melting away.

'You not being able to keep your hands off me was the whole point of wearing it,' she replied, laughing, the sound turning to a gasp as he turned her, his strong arms banding across her middle as they faced their reflection in the mirror.

Her need for him was painted all over her face. She had never been able to control it. There had been times when she could hide it, but now…now her longing was too big, too overpowering for her to exert any power over it. From the moment Domenico had started to dismantle his walls, she'd been lost to her desire completely. Lost to him. And she was sure he could see it too.

Eyes alight with a wicked kind of fever, he lowered his head to her neck and dusted her skin with light kisses, simultaneously moving his hand lower and lower, sliding it under the thin line of her panties in search of that bundle of exquisitely sensitive nerves. Pushing back her slick folds, he stroked a fingertip against her pulsing flesh, drawing a shattered sigh from her lips.

Domenico had always known how and where to touch her to make her scream, always seemed to sense how she wanted to be taken by him, but lately his touch had assumed a new power. It was reaching all the way into her, erasing her fears and caressing her soul. It was a way of being known that made her feel completely safe and yet utterly terrified.

Because surely that was everything one could hope to find in a lover. There was no greater connection, but if that was true… Rae was in even more dangerous territory than she'd thought. If only the danger wasn't so addictive.

Her mind sent into a spin by his touch, her head arched against his strong shoulder as his probing and caressing fingers sent the most magical, fluttering feelings unfurling within her like a flower responding to sunlight. The rhythm of sensations built, soaring higher and faster, and her knees were slackening with each beautifully torturous second that passed.

'Domenico,' she gasped out brokenly, unable to withstand it any longer.

'Open your eyes,' he commanded throatily. 'I want to watch you when you come.'

Rae hesitated. No doubt he had watched her orgasm before, but that was *then*. To do so now, to be looking into his eyes as she came apart under his caress would be extremely intimate and exposing, the forging of another deep connection, another unbreakable link between them, and that was the last thing she needed.

'Open your eyes for me, Rae. Let me see you.'

The silky murmur of his words worked their magic and, her resistance overridden, she slowly opened her eyes. The first thing she saw was his face, his eyes dark and commanding and fixed on her, ready to devour. She wanted to look away, look anywhere but at him, but she couldn't. With the devastating flash of his smile, Domenico sent his finger in a long, powerful stroke and that was all it took for Rae to implode, stars exploding behind her eyes and her whimpers filling the air around them.

His strong arms cradled her as she floated back down

to earth but hunger was still yawning inside her and so she turned, fastening her hands behind his head, pulling his mouth down and kissing him greedily, hoping to distract them both from her ecstasy, which had filled her expression.

Sex. It was just sex.

But the reminder felt hollow and so Rae poured everything into the kiss in a bid to prove it. Evidently as eager as her, Domenico's fingers moved to his shirt, ready to tear open the buttons, but Rae stilled his hand with her own.

'No. Let me,' she said, thrilled at the thought of undressing him, of revealing him inch by inch, the way she most loved.

Moving his hands away, Domenico stood still, breathing deeply as Rae smoothed her hands up to his broad shoulders and pushed his jacket off them, letting it fall to the floor. His eyes followed her every move and revelling in the freedom to touch him and determined to do to him what he had done to her, to make him feel as unsteady and exposed as she did, Rae traced the outline of his chest, her fingertips playing over the solid muscles and the hard ridges of his ribs. Each time she felt him quiver she danced her fingers a little further, her vulnerability diminishing with the thrill of feminine power rolling over her.

Had she ever before realised what she could do to him? Unsurprisingly, Domenico had always been the dominant sexual partner, but Rae was suddenly understanding that she had underestimated her power over him, that he was in thrall to her as well, and that was intoxicating…

She undid the buttons of his shirt slowly, one at a time, feeling his impatience mount, his breathing change as her fingers grazed purposefully against his bare skin. Once all the buttons were open, she pushed the sides of the shirt apart and pressed her lips to his warm chest. Domenico tensed and hissed beneath her, his fingers flexing at his sides as she teased a path of tender kisses down his hard stomach, following that line of faint dark hair that disappeared into the waistline of his trousers.

'Rae…' he groaned warningly as she neared the band of material, a plea she ignored to kiss her way back up his chest and manoeuvre him free from his shirt.

She tasted his lips again, her fingers continuing to roam across the planes of his upper body until his breathing was ragged and his chest was heaving and only then did she move her hands lower, unbuckling his belt, sliding down his fly and guiding his trousers and boxers down his strong legs.

And then he was completely naked, proud and erect before her eyes, and Rae had no desire to draw her gaze away. Only looking wasn't enough, not by a long shot. She needed to touch, to feel him, and so she pressed her hand against him, her body jolting in response.

When she felt him grow harder under her touch, that feeling only arrowed even deeper and her need to conquer even more of him, *all of him*, intensified to a treacherous degree…

Domenico couldn't comprehend what was happening. Sex with Rae had always been incredible, the best of his life, but he'd never been overpowered by those feelings. But as her hand slid slowly down his length, her touch consumed him in a way it never had before, blasting open everything inside him.

Lust. Desire. They were not powerful enough to describe the feelings unfolding within him and all he knew, all he could think, was that if he didn't have Rae back in his arms, back against his body in the next five seconds, he would implode.

Before she could act out her next intention, which Domenico read easily in her small, catlike smile, he clasped his hands to her hips and dragged her against him, seizing her mouth with a bruising, fevered kiss. Kicking his feet free from his trousers, he walked back towards the bed, bringing Rae tumbling down on top of him and keeping possession of her mouth, desperate to ease the hunger clamouring inside him, a hunger that seemed to emanate from the very centre of his being.

With her hair, her scent, her body, Rae surrounded him and that was driving him even crazier. No matter where he touched, how much sweetness he drank from her lips, it was not enough. Nothing satisfied the rushing of his blood, nothing helped him find that control that had always been present in his previous sexual encounters. That piece of himself that had always remained separate and safe. Untouched.

Reaching behind her, he tried to unclip her bra, but the force of his need was making his fingers unsteady and Rae had to help. Together they tossed the scrap of pretty lace aside and Domenico didn't waste a moment, taking the weight of her breasts in his hands and lifting his mouth to lick one and then the other, a worship that he had engaged in many times before, but that now felt different, more profound, for it was not just her body that he was adoring, but all of her. Her heart, her bravery, her passion. Everything that she had been generous enough to share with him and that he'd failed to appreciate for far too long, and her actions that night had clarified it even further.

His ministrations continuing with unrelenting expertise and feeding off the satisfied moans breaking from her lips, Domenico kissed the soft skin and sucked at her rosy nipples until she was writhing. That sight of her astride him, above him, her head thrown back as she fought the torrent of pleasure pulled a smile from his lips, but still, it wasn't enough.

An even darker, more urgent surge of passion rose up in him and with a single smooth movement Domenico flipped her over, trapping her under him. As he parted her legs, elation spread throughout his body and it startled him, as if he had finally found the place he recognised as home.

Rae was wet, as aroused as him, and for the first time in memory he couldn't hold back. He didn't even try, his actions being driven by a greater force than he could understand. He drove into her with ease, welcomed by her velvet heat, and the moment they joined together he felt something within him unlock. As if she was the solution to a problem, the answer to a code. It felt like the moment he had been waiting for, only he hadn't known it.

Trying to dislodge that unsettling poignancy, to focus only on the physical, Domenico started to move, following the urges of his body. Slowly he withdrew from her and then powered back inside, and Rae moved with those motions, her body sinuous and sensual against him. As they moved, she watched him from her bright eyes and, as their gazes held, he found he was incapable of looking away. Some new power within her gaze compelled him to maintain that connection and with each thrust of his body, with every answering lift of her hips, their eyes held, emotion starting to swirl amongst that physical tempest. Such fierce, unexpected emotion that Domenico could feel the last of his walls crumbling beneath its power, exposing everything that he was and leaving all of him open to her, to see and to take.

Beneath him, Rae began to shudder and as the tremors rocking her body spread into his own, the ripples of pleasure grew more powerful. They rushed through him so fast that they rammed into one another, becoming a single shattering orgasm that, for the first time in Domenico's life, left no single piece of him untouched.

CHAPTER TWELVE

'YOU ARE GOING to tell me where we're going at some point, aren't you?' Rae asked, smiling at the mysteriousness with which Domenico was acting.

'In about ninety seconds, you'll see for yourself,' he answered, at the exact moment the car drew to a stop.

They had arrived at a marina and as she saw what sat at the end of the dock Rae's eyes widened. The yacht had to be at least fifty feet long, with four levels, dazzlingly bright white against the darkening sky. The captain welcomed them as they stepped aboard, explaining that they would circle the island before introducing them to the crew, who were waiting to greet them with warm smiles and a glass of champagne.

As they pulled away from the dock, Domenico led Rae up to the third deck, where a tapas feast and a candlelit table for two was awaiting them.

'I cannot believe you did this,' Rae exclaimed when they were sitting at the table.

'We had to do something special to celebrate. With your help I finalised a very significant deal for The Ricci Group today.' Domenico had met with Lorca for two hours that morning and had returned to the villa with a completed contract and a triumphant mood. 'I only wish that Elena and Raphael could have been here to see it.'

'I have no doubt that wherever they are, Elena and Raphael are incredibly proud of you tonight.'

'I hope so,' he said quietly, a shadow scudding across his expression.

Rae's heart rippled with pain for him. 'You're still doubting yourself. Even after everything you've achieved today. You still think you have something to prove?'

'I've always felt it,' he admitted with a press of resignation to his lips. 'And I always think maybe if I do this, or if I achieve that...but nothing is ever enough to erase the feeling. I'm starting to think nothing will ever be the cure.'

'The cure is you, Domenico,' Rae beseeched him. 'You have to believe that you're deserving, that you're good enough. You have to ignore that voice that tells you you're lacking or worthless and trust that Elena would never have left you in charge of The Ricci Group if she didn't believe in you and trust you enormously. You have to believe that she loved you with all of her heart. I believe that. I saw it every time she looked at you. And you have to know that it doesn't matter one bit whether there is a piece of paper stuffed in some drawer that names you as her child or not.'

His eyebrows lifted, the slant of his gaze disbelieving, and Rae wished so badly that she could make him see that his belonging and his worth were defined by so much more than a completed form.

'In every way that mattered, you were Elena's son. It

was you who had dinner with her every Sunday night. It was you who went with her to her hospital appointments. It was you she turned to when she had a problem. That is what belonging to someone is about. All those small, everyday acts. Not a name on your birth certificate.'

Domenico nodded, but he could hide little from her now and the flatness of his mouth, the way he cast his eyes down was telling.

'But it's not just that, is it?' Rae deduced. 'It's not just your mother leaving you and Elena not adopting you… What else happened?'

Pain flashed like lightning across his handsome face and for a split second Raw saw, to her shock, all the anguish that he had so adeptly hidden from her. It was right there on the surface.

'She had other children. My mother,' he stated in a voice breaking with repressed emotion. 'The reason she moved to Venice was because she got married and they had children—children whose births she announced and celebrated, welcoming them into her life in the way she never did with me. She even had stepchildren whom she happily accepted. And I was…ignored. I watched it all… watched her embrace those babies, giving them the security of family and parents…and each time I saw them I found myself asking what was so wrong with me that she hadn't kept me. Why I was so *unlovable*.' He shook his head, emitting a low curse in his native tongue. 'I shouldn't have cared. I had Elena and she gave me her name and a home, protection I would never have had. It shouldn't have hurt me.'

'Of course it should,' Rae reassured him, reaching

out to curl her hand around his tense arm. 'You're not wrong to be hurt by what happened. Anyone would be.'

Rae's throat was clogged as she considered what those circumstances must have been like for him. Watching from afar, having that same bruise pressed upon day after day.

'You'd think I would have been smart enough to learn my lesson that day she looked right through me. But I wasn't. I went to her home once, to try and meet her.'

'What happened?' Rae asked, almost holding her breath, because she knew by the hollow look in his eyes that it had left a wound.

'I'm sure you can imagine.'

She nodded. 'I can. But I think you should tell me anyway. Then maybe you can let it go.'

'I knocked on the door and an older couple answered. Her parents, my grandparents. It was the first time I'd ever seen them, but I think they knew who I was straight away. I introduced myself and a look of such contempt came across both of their faces. I told them I wanted to see my mother, they refused. They said that she wasn't my mother, she'd never wanted anything to do with me, that I was a no one even if Elena had given me her name, that I was nothing more than a mutt and none of them wanted anything to do with me. Then they hissed at me to leave and never come back and slammed the door in my face.'

Rae gave a small shake of her head. To have experienced such cruelty from people who should have loved and cared for him. Accepted him.

'But that wasn't even the worst part. As I backed

away, I looked up at the house and I saw her—my mother—watching from a window. She'd known I was there, she'd heard everything they said and did nothing. She just looked right through me again before turning away. Like I really was nothing.' He smiled grimly. 'I've never told anyone about that before.'

Was that when it had started, Rae wondered, his habit of burying everything so deep so he could pretend it had never happened? How it all must have festered in him, turning every thought dark and black and hopeless, making him worry that every relationship would end with a closed door.

'There's no way to defend their actions, but I will say this about your mother. She was only very young when she had you and if her parents weren't supportive that can't have been easy. So maybe when she left you on Elena's doorstep she knew she was leaving you with someone who would take care of you, the way she wanted you to be taken care of. Maybe that was an act of loving you.' She saw by his expression that he was listening. And hearing. 'And maybe…maybe when she saw you again, well…'

'Maybe she had consigned that to a box that she didn't want to open either,' Domenico offered, finishing her thought with a sigh of willing acceptance.

'It's possible. But what I know for sure is that you're definitely not nothing, Domenico. Your grandparents could not have been more wrong. You are remarkable. You're intelligent and generous and kind. You stepped up when Elena needed you to. You've spent every day of your adult life honouring her and Raphael's legacy. Those are the actions of a wonderful man.'

'It's a little strange to hear the wife who walked out on me declaring how wonderful I am,' he remarked with dry humour, but beneath that veneer Rae heard his vulnerability. Saw the hurt etching itself into his profile in spite of his efforts to hold it back.

And for the first time she could see the far-reaching consequences of her hasty, panicked decision to quit their marriage. Could see how that had cut to the deepest part of him, inflicting a fresh wound over an old one. And she knew she could no longer withhold what truly lay at the core of that decision—the truth of her mother's passing. She had let it remain a secret for too long and now that Domenico had taken the monumental step of laying his soul completely bare, Rae had to find the courage to do the same. She had to be as brave and vulnerable as he had been. Only then would he be able to understand everything about her, and she knew what a beautiful gift that was.

'I didn't leave because I thought you weren't good enough, Domenico,' she admitted, steeling herself with a quick breath because she knew there was no going back from this moment. 'I left because of me. Because I was scared.'

'Scared?' Domenico repeated, unmoving as he absorbed her confession and tried frantically to make sense of it. 'Of what?'

Colour drained from her face and she scraped her

teeth over her lower lip before answering. 'Of being like my mother.'

Domenico frowned in confusion, her words making no sense to him. 'Explain,' he commanded softly.

Rae took a small breath, glancing off to the side, but she wasn't quick enough to hide the sheen of tears coating her gaze. 'When my dad died, my mum gave up completely. Her whole life had revolved around him and with him gone, she didn't know who she was. Each day that passed, she slid deeper and deeper into a depression that none of us could pull her from.'

'I thought she died of pneumonia,' he queried gently, trying to assemble all these new facts into the right order.

Rae gave a small, stiff nod, meeting his eyes for only the tiniest moment. 'She did. She got caught outside in a storm without a coat and she caught a chill that went straight to her chest and eventually ended up in hospital. But she shouldn't have been outside...' She hesitated, her face filling with a ravaged kind of hurt. 'She wasn't strong enough. Since he'd passed, she'd barely eaten, barely slept, her weight had fallen off her. She was like a ghost.'

He moved closer to her, wanting to offer comfort with his presence, the promise that she was safe from that past. Seeing the tremble of her body, he slid his jacket from his shoulders and draped it over hers.

'It was awful, Domenico. Watching her waste away like that. Day after day. And I couldn't do anything. Then, when I realised how empty my life was in Venice, all I could think was that the same thing was going to happen to me, and I couldn't let that happen. I couldn't follow her down that path. I couldn't put Maggie and Imogen through that agony all over again, put myself through it.'

He pulled her into his arms, holding her securely against his chest as her body shook with emotion. Not only did he ache for the losses she had suffered, but for the agony she'd had to go through in watching it happen and being powerless to stop it. He hated that he hadn't known any of it before that moment, that in attempting to keep his pain buried, he had forced Rae to be silent about her own. He knew nothing good came from keeping pain boxed inside, but at no point in time had he considered it was his role as her husband to try and tease her secrets from their hiding place, but it was not a new realisation that as a husband he had focused on all the wrong things. On formalising her position as his wife, on gifting her jewellery and various other material luxuries, but not what she'd really needed and wanted. A husband attentive enough to know that she was battling a deep-rooted fear, a husband who would listen and share in return, a husband who'd make the effort to find out her needs and prioritise them.

But he was no longer in the dark. He understood why she had left him, why she'd felt it had been her only choice. Why she had seen no future in their marriage.

That she trusted him enough now to tell him her truth, after everything, was incredible. Obviously, he had somehow managed to start to restore the connection that had once bound them together, but it burned him to know that he could have known these truths sooner and spared them both a mountain of pain. If only he hadn't been so intent on keeping their relationship as a primarily physical connection, so scared of going any deeper than the surface and dislodging everything that lay below. If only he had done as Elena had urged and gone after Rae the second she'd left. He should have chased her to London and banged on her door and refused to leave until she'd talked to him. *Dios*, it was what a large part of him had strained to do…but he had been too proud. And too scared.

It had been too easy to believe that she'd deserted him because she didn't love him any more. Too easy to recall his past and heed those dark thoughts that rose in his mind like smoke. He'd let himself be convinced that all that awaited him in London was a closed door and another rejection and had idiotically fallen prey to that fear of not being enough.

Although Rae had been the one to leave him, Domenico knew now that he was the reason she had stayed lost to him.

Rae was right. He needed to silence those ugly thoughts in his head. He needed to look to what he knew to be true in his heart and trust that or he would be doomed to stumble again and again over that same fear.

Holding on to her tighter, he pressed his lips to the top of her head and inhaled that light scent she always carried with her. She drew back slightly, pressing her hands to his chest and looking up at him.

'Surely you see now it was as much to do with me as it was you. And if I'd had any idea what that my leaving would make you think…' She stopped, raising a hand to his face, her warm palm curling around his cheek, a touch of such tenderness he found himself leaning into it. 'You're not unlovable, Domenico,' she whispered, gazing up at him with all the magic of the stars above reflected in her eyes. 'You're the furthest thing from it.'

Her words held such feeling and such quiet power that the only thing he could do in that moment was claim her lips and it was a kiss that contained everything. Joy and passion. Forgiveness. But also regret and sorrow. Because, as badly as they wished it, neither of them could change what had happened, their many mistakes and the many hurts.

And yet, amongst all that wreckage, there was a single revelation sticking in Domenico's mind. That Rae had never stopped loving him, and that made his heart feel fuller than it had in a very long time.

CHAPTER THIRTEEN

Rae woke from her sleep with a jolt.

Her skin was sticky and her heart was pounding, a hot and sickly panic gushing through her veins.

She lay still, waiting for the threat of the dream to fade, for her breathing to settle into a more even rhythm, for the drumbeat of fear to grow smaller and shallower and her limbs to unfreeze and, as soon as she was able, she swept the covers aside, casting a quick look at Domenico to make sure he was still sound asleep before carefully extracting herself from his tight embrace and slipping out of the bed and the room.

Her feet carried her down the stairs and outside and she welcomed the waft of the cool, clean morning air against her face and the feel of the sand beneath her feet as she walked across their private horseshoe-shaped beach towards the gentle froth of the waves.

Taking a seat on the sand, Rae hugged her knees up to her chest and rested her chin on her knees, her mind going back to her dream. No, not a dream—her nightmare. It was one she'd had before, but not for many months. In it she was lost, casting around for any kind of anchor or raft to grab on to, but there was nothing apart from an encroaching blackness, looming thick and dark and growing even greater the nearer it came. It was blinding and choking, strangling her screams and sucking her in, no matter how hard she fought it, until it was all around her, taking her over, pulling her down. That was when she'd woken up. That was always when she woke up.

Pulling her knees in tighter, Rae sucked in a shuddery breath of air, feeling the surge of a fresh wave of panic. Because she knew exactly what that dream was about, and she knew exactly why she'd had it again.

Because of last night. Those emotional, transforming few hours in which everything had changed.

Everything.

She and Domenico had become closer than they had ever been before. Closer than she had ever felt to another person, than she'd ever believed it was possible to be.

There was nothing standing between them now. Nothing pushing them apart or holding them back. There was just the two of them, their defences lowered and their hearts open. Together, they had ripped down the last few walls that had stood between them and dragged all of their secrets and fears into the light, but what had endowed those moments with even more power, even more meaning, was that they had *chosen* to do that. Individually, they had each decided to be more honest than they'd ever previously been, decided that they wanted the other person to know all of their heart as if they had been holding it in their hands. That they had both found themselves in that same place at the same time, both of them filled with courage and willing, seemed to Rae to be incredibly beautiful and incredibly poignant.

All she had ever wanted was for them to be reading from the same page, and for the first time in a very long time they were.

And with every new piece of himself that Domenico had revealed to her, Rae had fallen more and more in love with him. Because, with his whole story out in the open, she was able to see how strong and determined and noble he truly was.

She'd always been in awe of his strength, that ability he possessed to carry everything and even more on his very broad shoulders, but knowing that he'd been rejected and abandoned and broken and was still upstanding in spite of that was mesmeric. That he had found the perseverance to go on, to retain the trust he had in Elena, and to believe in Rae enough to want to marry her, spoke volumes about his capacity to feel and the fact that didn't understand how remarkable he was only made Rae's love for him so much greater.

But that meant her fear was that much bigger too.

Because the love she was feeling—the fierce, intense, passionate devotion to him—was anchored too deep and consumed too much of her. It had the power to be utterly devastating and that was terrifying.

It was a risk that Rae wasn't sure she could live with.

She knew too well what followed devastation. The darkness. The swallowing, surrounding, smothering darkness, which had been hunting her in her dream. The one that she feared coming for her in reality, just as it had preyed on her beautiful, strong mother. And as long as she loved Domenico as much as she did, that was a worry that she would carry with her each and every day. What if she lost him? How would she cope? Would she even be able to?

As those questions mounted, a cavern opened in her stomach, filling with the bitterest kind of dread, so strong that she could suddenly taste it in her mouth. And all she wanted to do was run. Run fast and far and away from all of those feelings.

As much as Rae had loved her mother, she didn't want to follow in her footsteps. She didn't want to force her sisters to watch another person they loved suffer and there was no way for her to reel in her feelings. They were too powerful, with a force of their own. Intense. Enthralling. That was the way it had always been between her and Domenico. She didn't believe it could be any other way. Their love had been forged in the sizzling flames of their instant, scorching passion, and the many ways they had opened up to each other in recent days had only fanned those flames.

It was everything that Rae had once wanted with him. A soul-deep, unshakeable, unbreakable bond… but back then she hadn't known how deep that fear was anchored in her, hadn't fully comprehended the consequences of such a connection. The power and sway it held over her. Now she did, and she knew those consequences could be catastrophic, and that scared her more than she could say.

She didn't want to live with fear shadowing her every move. She didn't want to feel fragile every minute of every day, worrying about what lurked around the corner. It had been hard enough last time and even with all the work she had done to make herself strong, to make her life fuller and become more robust so that nothing could ever break her the way her mum had been broken, it wasn't enough. Nothing was powerful enough to counter Domenico's presence and power over her. She still felt vulnerable and afraid.

Too vulnerable. *Too* afraid.

She felt it when she spotted Domenico striding across the beach to join her, felt it as she watched him work on the plane going home to Venice, his head bent low as he typed out email after email, occasionally looking up to send her one of his slow, devastating smiles, and she felt it when he kissed her goodbye at the airport before he went off in one direction to the Ricci offices and she returned to the palazzo.

Every time she looked at him, she felt that overpowering wave of love for the man he had become in spite of everything he had had to endure. And then a deep, threatening stab of fear.

It was a relief to have some space from him and some time to herself, a few hours without that frantic back and forth of feeling. But once back at the palazzo Rae became restless, unable to settle peacefully to even the smallest of tasks, and so when, mid-afternoon, her phone rang with an incoming video call from Nell, she leapt to answer it, eager for the distraction that a friendly conversation would provide.

'I have some very exciting news for you,' Nell announced after they'd exchanged pleasantries, launching into a description of the conversation she'd had with the owner of New York's biggest and world-famous bridal boutique.

'Are you serious?' Rae gasped in disbelief when Nell had finished. 'They want to stock my dresses? Even though there aren't even samples of all my designs yet, only sketches?'

'They like what they see,' Nell said, beaming at her through the screen. 'It also doesn't hurt that your name is quickly becoming one of the hottest new names in bridal design. And they don't just want to stock your dresses, Rae. They want to have your designs exclusively and offer their brides a custom service with you. It will be like having your own boutique within their store.'

Rae gave a gob-smacked laugh and lifted her hands to her mouth. 'That's incredible. I can't believe it. I... I'm speechless.'

'It's a huge opportunity, Rae. An unbelievable one. And with all the hard work you've done recently, you really do deserve it. So how do you feel about coming and living in New York for a while?'

Rae opened her mouth to reply, but no words came out. Because the reality of the offer was only just sinking in, the understanding that accepting it meant relocating. To New York.

New York. It had always seemed like such a frenetic and overwhelming place to her, never a city that she'd longed to visit, but that wasn't the foremost thought in her mind. No, at the centre of her mind was Domenico. The heart-slowing realisation that if she was in New York, she wouldn't, *couldn't*, be with him because his life was in Venice.

And although excitement was absolutely what she should be feeling, how could she feel any excitement in her heart about being somewhere he wasn't, when her heart so completely belonged to him?

'I don't know,' she stammered on a nervous laugh, realising her silence had dragged on a little too long. 'I guess I'm a little taken aback. It's a lot to take in.'

'I know.' Nell nodded sympathetically. 'It would be a big change for you. But they wouldn't be looking for you to be in New York until some time after the New Year, so nothing would happen immediately. You and Domenico would have plenty of time to figure things out,' she offered as an attempt at reassurance. 'But, if you are interested, the owners would like to meet with you as soon as this week, just to talk through all the particulars and start the process moving. So think about it. It really is an incredible opportunity for you, Rae.'

'I know,' Rae managed, her throat growing tighter by the second. 'I'll talk to you later, okay.'

Ending the call, she dropped the phone onto the desk and sat back in her chair, her teeth nibbling on the inside of her lip as thoughts sifted through her mind at a mile a minute.

It was, as Nell had said, an incredible offer. Perhaps a once-in-a-lifetime opportunity. And it would give Rae everything she wanted. Success. Security. Something that could sustain her should the worst ever happen. There would be no need for her to worry any longer about falling into that black abyss. She should be thrilled, overjoyed. A month ago, she knew she would have leapt to accept it without a second thought, but now…now there was Domenico to think about too.

There was her and Domenico.

They had finally reached the place in their relationship that she had always wanted, she thought, her heart racing with renewed feeling. They were poised on the edge of their own opportunity to start over and, as frightening as that was, as much as she had spent all day fretting about it, there was a part of Rae that wanted exactly that. To spend her life with him. To build a family with him. To be there when he was struggling, to share in his success and share hers with him. Everything meant so much more with him. Just last night she had fallen asleep with images of the life they could build together swimming before her eyes.

She believed wholeheartedly that they could make their marriage successful this time. They had both grown so much, changed in so many ways, big and small, that she had no doubt that they could make their lives together work, managing their marriage and their careers.

But if she went to New York, none of that would be possible. Everything between them would be severed. The possibility, the hope, the connection they had both fought to forge.

But you wouldn't have to live in fear of losing him, you wouldn't have to feel scared and vulnerable. You'd feel strong and safe and successful.

Her heart skipped several beats, tempted by that possibility, except…

She wouldn't have Domenico and if she didn't have

Domenico, she wouldn't have her heart. She would only be half alive.

A glimmer of movement caught the corner of her eye and Rae looked up, her heart ramming straight into her ribs as she saw Domenico's reflection in the mirror, standing in the doorway.

For the longest moment she was frozen, a thudding fear pulsing behind her breastbone as she stared at him, trying desperately to read his face, to gauge how much he had heard and what thoughts were running through his mind. Had he already jumped to the conclusion that he was being abandoned again? Was that why his face was set that way, so flat and unreadable, his eyes as dark as night? Were his wounds tearing themselves open again?

She turned quickly. 'How long have you been standing there?'

He didn't move, and that stillness strummed at her nerves, making them jangle with ominous feeling. 'Long enough.'

She swallowed. 'Did you hear all of my conversation with Nell?'

'Most of it, yes.'

It was difficult to speak over the panic hammering in her throat and chest, but she managed to do so. She took a slow step towards him, scared of moving too quickly, as if he were an animal that could startle.

'Then you know I didn't commit to anything. I wouldn't do that without talking to you.'

'Nell said the job wouldn't begin until the New Year,' he said without any inflection and that flatness made her unease mount even higher. 'Our arrangement ends well before Christmas, Rae. You don't need my agreement on whatever you do after that.'

She blinked, stunned by his words. Why he was saying that? As if her future was no concern of his, of no interest to him? It made no sense to her, especially not after everything they'd shared last night, after the beautiful way they had given all of themselves to one another and in doing so blasted open a door to their future.

'I don't need it, no,' she agreed, frowning and picking her following words with care. 'But I would like it. I would like to talk about it with you. To know where you stand, how you feel.'

To know that you love me as much as I love you. To know that you are in this as deeply as I am and that you want me to stay and be your wife. To know that you believe we can make our relationship work this time, that you too believe we are stronger and better than the people we were before.

He looked at her directly, but the eyes staring back at her did not belong to the man she had come to know over the past seventy-two hours. Not the eyes that had looked deep into hers as he had moved slowly inside her last night, sealing their emotional bond with the sharpest and sweetest physical joining of her life. Not the eyes of the man who had stroked her hair back from her face as they'd lain face to face afterwards.

'I think you should accept the offer and go to New York,' he responded without a single beat of hesitation, and Rae could only stare back at him harder, nonplussed and sure, *certain*, that she had misheard him.

* * *

Domenico thought that saying the words would break him. That forcing them out of his mouth would cause him to shatter into pieces, or at least be struck by a bolt of lightning because they were such a big lie. But they flowed from his lips without a single tremor and, once they had, he felt a brief sense of relief, because he knew the hardest part was over. He had started down the path. Now he just had to keep going.

Because he owed Rae this. The freedom to follow her rainbow to the end and find the success and happiness that awaited her there. It was what she wanted, after all. What she wanted—and needed—more than anything. And he had denied her too much and failed her in too many ways already to allow her to turn down the opportunity.

For a large part of the day that was all he had been able to think about—the poor husband he'd been. Grappling with a profound sense of guilt, Domenico had questioned if his mistakes would be too great to be overcome, if his and Rae's past would prevent them from reaching the brighter future he knew with absolute unflinching certainty that he wanted with her. He'd known it as soon as he'd woken that morning, drained from his emotional outpouring of the night before, but with that weight of the past lifted from him, all the murkiness and insecurity bled out of him, he'd felt a freedom and clarity unlike anything he'd known before. And his every thought, every skip of his heart, had been for Rae.

He loved her. He always had. He'd just been so lost in the darkness of his thoughts that he hadn't been able to realise it. Elena had been right. Rae was the only one for him. She did make him the best version of himself. She had healed him. Because of her, standing beside him the whole time, telling him it was okay, reminding him that he was safe, assuring him that he was not what he feared, he had finally found the strength to face his painful past and at long last been able to view it, not through the eyes of a shaken and hurt little boy, but a man who understood that people were complex and flawed.

Because of Rae, he finally understood that love was not contained in a single act of claiming or acceptance. It was something that was given and felt day in, day out in a thousand small ways. And, adopted by her or not, that was the way Elena had loved him. And the way Rae had loved him too.

Beautiful, wonderful, incredible Rae.

It was because of how wonderful she was that he knew he had to say those words again and tell her to go to New York. Because it was what she deserved, but she was so generous of heart and so used to putting others before herself that she was already hesitating to seize it.

Because of them. *Him.*

He'd listened to her reaction to the news, heard her uncertainty about relocating to New York, and with a sharp twist of his heart and gut had realised that she was veering on the edge of turning the offer down. And he couldn't allow her to do that.

Rae had already sacrificed so much for him. She had given up everything she'd ever known and worked for to start a life with him in Venice, a sacrifice that he hadn't appreciated at the time, but he did now. And then she had denied her own wants and needs so as not to upset him.

Standing in her way again was not an option. He couldn't do it. He *wouldn't*.

No matter how much he wanted to hold on tight to her, to keep her with him for ever, never again would he be the one to hold her back, not when the emotional cost to her would be so very high.

'I'm sorry, I don't think I heard you correctly,' Rae breathed out quickly.

Domenico knew that she had heard him, but he repeated himself anyway, forcing himself to ignore that pain in her blue eyes and the weight hurting his chest.

'I said that I think you should accept the job in New York.'

She looked bewildered, her forehead creasing, her eyes crinkling as they narrowed disbelievingly. 'Why are saying that?'

'Because you asked for my opinion. And that's what I think you should do. It sounds like it's an amazing opportunity for you.'

'But if I take it, it would mean I would be living in New York, Domenico. Permanently. I wouldn't be here. We…we wouldn't be able to be together.'

Domenico kept a tight check on his emotions. He had to, or the words he really wanted to say would spill right out of him. Only he couldn't let that happen. He couldn't dwell on the empty landscape that awaited him without her. He had to let her go. Whatever that meant for him afterwards was something he would just have to deal with.

He nodded blankly. 'I understand. But we won't be together in the New Year anyway. We'll be divorced by then, remember?' he said, his voice cool and calm and sounding like it belonged to someone else. 'Our arrangement only lasts for six months, Rae.'

'Our arrangement?' she exclaimed. 'Domenico, nothing that has happened in the last few days has been about the stupid charade I agreed to! The things we've shared with each other, everything we talked about last night—that was all real. You can't tell me it didn't mean anything, that it hasn't altered anything between us.'

'No, I won't deny that,' he agreed. 'Last night changed many things. I think we understand one another far better than we ever did. But one night doesn't fix a broken-down marriage, *tesoro*. And if last night revealed anything, it's that we both want and need different things from a relationship. Things we can't get from each other.'

She was shaking her head indignantly, colour rising in her cheeks, and she was all the more beautiful for it. He longed to reach out, place his fingers against her skin, feel that delicious combination of silk and heat.

'No. You don't mean that,' she whispered. And then in a stronger voice, 'I don't believe you.'

'Have you ever known me to say anything that I don't mean, Rae?' he parried calmly.

'So that's just it?' she demanded of him. 'None of this has meant anything to you? You're just happy to walk away from this? From us?'

He shoved his hands into his pockets, to keep himself from reaching out for her, and faced her with a sigh.

'There is no us, Rae. Our marriage stopped being real a long time ago. This has just been a way to…close the door for good.'

It was in that moment that she faltered, his purposely cruel words cracking her spirit and her willingness to fight. He watched the colour in her eyes and cheeks fade, watched her start to splinter inside, and he wanted so badly to go to her, but he held himself firm. Held himself back. Weakening was not an option, not when her happiness was at stake.

'You're right. I don't know what I was thinking.' She looked away, placing a hand against her chest. 'If you'll excuse me, I would like to be alone. I need to call Nell back and make arrangements for my trip to New York.'

Nodding and turning away, Domenico sucked in a silent breath that caused his heart and lungs to burn. He'd achieved what he wanted, but there was no sense of triumph in it, only misery.

CHAPTER FOURTEEN

RAE KNEW HER flight to New York would be boarding soon, so she cleared away the wrapper from her sandwich and, after a last glance at her phone, tucked it safely away in her bag. In ten hours she would be in Manhattan, building her plans for her future. A future that didn't involve Domenico.

Her heart squeezed, the pain so acute that she felt it everywhere, but she breathed through it, knowing that leaving was for the best. This way, she would be safe and secure, taking a big step towards making herself invulnerable.

And Domenico didn't want her anyway.

'There is no us, Rae. This has just been a way to... close the door for good.'

The memory of those words carved through her, almost as cold and sharp as the first time. With them, he had made it clear where he stood, the sentiment rolling off his tongue without a single beat of hesitation.

Do you really believe that, Rae? That he doesn't care for you? You know what you felt in his arms and saw glowing in his eyes—do you truly think that was all a lie? Or did you just accept the escape that he was offer-ing because it was all becoming a bit too real, too scary?

Rae tried to swat away the thought, but it stuck, forc-ing her to examine its veracity and grudgingly acknowl-edge what motivations had driven her actions. She had been scared in that moment, standing at that crossroads that would set the tone for the following years of her life, a crossroads she hadn't expected to come to, especially not so swiftly. But she would have chosen Domenico. She had wanted to choose him.

Then why didn't you? Why didn't you fight back against his words and tell him how much you love him and that you wanted to stay with him?

Because…a baseball-sized lump formed in her throat.

Because of fear. Because, faced with her rupturing heart and the pain exploding in every corner of her body, it had been easier to not fight. To accept his words, his rejection, and let it all go.

You promised to not be a coward any more.

Rae hissed out a breath, frustration with herself burn-ing deep within, making her feel all twisted up inside. She had let fear win, allowed it to dictate her actions, and if she kept going, if she got on her flight, she would still be running, and not towards something she wanted, but away from something she was scared to want.

In that second, she knew what she needed to do.

She had to go back. She had to tell Domenico ex-actly how she felt, one final act of vulnerability, and probably the hardest one. But she had to do it. Her fear would never go away completely. With love there would always be fear. But if she faced it, it would shrink and its power over her would lessen. And maybe, in leading by example and putting her heart in Domenico's hands, he would feel safe enough to put his in hers and conquer whatever it was that had made him hold back.

And if he didn't love her, if everything he had said the other night was the truth, then Rae would just have to live with it. She wouldn't be scared of that and she wouldn't allow herself to fall apart, because she was strong and she was brave. She might not always remember that when she needed to, but that was who she was. Strong and brave, and it was time she started acting like it.

Overhead, the speakers flared into life, announcing that her flight was ready to board, but she was already on her feet and hurrying in the opposite direction, towards the exit. And, hopefully, towards love.

Domenico was relieved when the meeting was over.

His head hadn't been in it. More than once he'd had to be prompted to answer a question that had been asked of him and that he hadn't heard as he was too busy thinking about Rae, wondering where she was and what she was doing at that very moment, if she was missing him as profoundly as he was missing her. Not that that was likely, not after the words he'd spoken in their last conversation. But he'd had to make her leave and he hadn't known any other way to do that.

Rising from his chair at the head of the long table, he knew he needed to get his thoughts in order before his conference call later that afternoon. To focus on the matters at hand. But it was a struggle.

He'd made a bad habit of stuffing his feelings down and never dealing with them and he didn't want to do that any more, not after realising how all those unresolved emotions had festered in him like a contagion. He wanted to be better, to manage his emotions with more maturity so they didn't constrain and control him as those childhood ones had, but allowing himself to feel his pain was agonising.

More than once he'd noted the time on his watch, calculated that he had time to race to the airport and stop Rae, tell her he hadn't meant any of what he had said and plead with her to stay, but then his better sense overrode that emotion and for the hundredth time he sternly reminded himself that he had let Rae go for a reason, and a good reason at that—because of what was best for her, and that was a life with her career at the centre of it.

Are you sure you weren't pushing her away more than letting her go?

Domenico wanted to reject the thought out of hand, but the twist of his gut forced him to concede that, yes, maybe he had been pushing Rae away to a certain extent. Because embarking on a future with her would require him to trust that he could be enough for her. A good enough man and a good enough husband, who wouldn't screw up as epically as he had last time. And trusting in that, *in himself*, was not easy...not after everything he'd been through, all those years of pervasive doubt and insecurity. It lingered like a decaying stench and when faced with that very big question mark about their future, about his ability to give her a good future, that fear had blown up in his mind and he had reacted to it. Because he couldn't bear to cause Rae pain again. To be the reason she was unhappy. He could think of no worse fate.

As he strode back to his office, Domenico passed his assistant at his desk. 'I don't want to be bothered for the next hour, Nico. No exceptions,' he commanded wearily, sensing that Nico had words on his lips, but closing his office door before he could get them out.

He leaned back against the door, closing his eyes and giving himself a moment to buckle under the magnitude of his pain.

'Having a bad day?'

His eyes snapped open. Sitting in his chair, behind his desk and looking right at him with her bright blue eyes was Rae. He blinked quickly, making sure he wasn't imagining her.

'You're meant to be on a plane on your way to New York right now,' he managed, his voice hoarse.

'I know, but the thing is, Domenico, I don't want to go to New York.'

His heart stuttered. *She didn't want to go?*

'But the job with the bridal store—it's a huge…'

'It's a huge opportunity, I know,' she sighed, as though she was tired of hearing those words. 'But I'm not sure it's the right one, not if it means leaving you.' Words failed him, especially as she pressed herself out of his chair and moved around the desk towards him, her footsteps sure, her eyes fixed steadily on him. 'I love you, Domenico. I love you with every breath that I take and I want to be your wife now even more than I did when you first asked me to marry you. Knowing exactly who you are has only made everything I feel for you stronger and I want spend the rest of my life with you.'

The sparkle of her eyes intensified, the truth of her words easy to see, and his heart quivered, threatening to burst open with the delight streaming into it. 'The only reason I even set that meeting for New York was because I was scared of everything that I was feeling, scared of the fear that comes with loving you so much, and when you told me *repeatedly* to go, I thought, okay, maybe it's better this way. This way, I won't have to live with that fear of making the same mistakes as my mum. But I realised that I was only making a different one. Because, by trying so hard to not be like her, I was going to the other extreme—a life without love, a life controlled by fear. And that's not what I want either. Because a life without you just isn't a life.'

She moved closer, hope brimming in her face. 'What I do want is to stay here and be your wife. Not just for a few months, but for ever. And I know it won't be easy, making our marriage work with both of our careers, it will take a lot of work, but I believe in us enough to know that we can.'

He moved like a bullet, darting towards her and taking her face in his hands, kissing her long and slow and stopping only because there were some words he needed to say. 'I want you to stay too, Rae,' he murmured breathlessly, the words in a rush to get out. 'I only told you to go because I didn't want to stand in your way again. I didn't want to be the reason you would one day wake up unhappy. But telling you to leave nearly killed me. I've been in a fog ever since.'

'That is the most selfless, sexy and stupid thing you've ever done for me. And I forbid you to ever do something like that again,' she said strictly, but with a dazzling smile up at him. 'We need to be honest with each other if we're going to make this work, Domenico. We have to always tell each other what we're thinking and feeling, however hard it is, however scared we are that the other won't like what they have to hear.'

'I'm scared that I can't be enough for you,' he admitted roughly, not wanting to hold anything back from her. 'That, however hard I try, I won't ever be the man you deserve.'

She reached up her hand to his face and cupped his jaw with her warm palm, empathy shining out of her eyes because she knew exactly why he thought that without him having to say anything more. 'You're already everything I want, Domenico. I'll tell you that every day if you need me to. And as for you standing in my way—you're not. I'm making a considered decision about what I do and don't want. That's different to how it was last time. And New York is just one opportunity. Hopefully, there will be others and when they come we'll talk about them. If we can make it work and how we do that.'

'I actually already have a thought about that,' Domenico said, detaching from her reluctantly and moving to his desk, withdrawing a file from his top drawer. 'For you,' he said, placing it in her hands and watching as she opened it and withdrew the sheets of paper inside, a puzzled look racing over her expression.

'You bought me a building?'

'A three-storey building on the corner of Salizada San Moisè, so lots of windows, lots of beautiful natural light. I thought, to start with, it would be a good studio. You could bring brides there for consultations and fittings and then, eventually, the ground floor could be a store. Your first store.'

She looked overcome, her eyes moving from him to the paper and back to him. 'I… I can't believe you did this.'

'I had Nico start looking after our conversation on the plane to Majorca. I wanted to do something for you, to make everything up to you. And to show you how much I believe in you and support you.' He slid his arms around her waist, drawing her against him. 'I didn't always in the past, but I do now and I will every day going forward. Because I love you. More than anything.'

He rested his forehead against hers, contentment sinking down the length of his body. 'You're my home, Rae. You are where I belong. And we will make this work. I will not allow anything to come between us ever again.'

She smiled up at him, the words bringing palpable relief to her body. 'And I won't run any more, I promise. Whatever problem or fear I have, I will come to you.'

'And I will always make time to listen and be there for you and whatever it is that you need, I'll make sure you have it.'

'Right now—' she smiled, sliding her hands up his chest and around his neck '—I think I already have everything I need.'

'As do I, Signora Ricci,' he said, smiling that long, slow, devastating smile. 'As long as I have you, I am complete.'

EPILOGUE

Three years later

THE RICCI BALL WAS in full swing. It had become one of the biggest nights in Venice's social calendar and the gilded ballroom was packed with guests. The chandelier high above glittered in splendour, rare jewels sparkled at every table, but as far as Domenico was concerned, nothing and no one shone as brightly as his wife. As his eyes found her among the throng, he cut an eager path towards her.

'Are you having a good time?' he whispered, slipping his hands around her stomach and resting them on her protruding bump, which even her cleverly designed dress couldn't completely hide.

'Yes. But it's even better now that you're back at my side,' she murmured, stroking a hand across his jaw.

'Would you like to dance?'

'As if you need to ask. I told you I want to make the most of tonight before I'm too big to do anything…'

'You'll still be ravishing,' Domenico cut in.

'And before these babies get here and drastically upend our lives.'

The pregnancy had been planned entirely, but the news that it was a double pregnancy had stunned both of them. It had taken Rae a little time to adjust to the idea.

He smiled down at her, pulling her in close. 'I think we're going to handle it fine. We'll do it the way we do everything—together.'

It was how they had navigated the whirlwind that the past few years had been, juggling both of their busy careers and their marriage. The Ricci Group had continued to flourish, with the maiden voyage of their cruise line setting sail a month earlier to a hail of praise, and Rae's career had gone from strength to strength. She had opened her first store in Venice two years ago, in the building Domenico had gifted her, drawing in brides from all across Europe, but as her renown had grown, so had the global demand for her bridal gowns. Partnering with a high-end department store in a deal facilitated by Domenico, six months ago she had opened her first boutique in their London store, with a second one set to open in New York in four months' time. It hadn't always been easy, but with communication and love they had managed it, their marriage growing stronger than ever.

'I love you, Domenico Ricci. My life wouldn't be complete without you.'

'You're everything to me, *mi amore*. And I can't wait to meet our two babies and tell them how perfect and how loved they are.'

Seven weeks later, Domenico was able to do exactly that. Their newborn daughters arrived several weeks early, but thankfully healthy. They named them Elena and Raphaella, names he and Rae had agreed upon very easily, and cradling them in his arms for the first time, Domenico murmured to them just how loved and precious they were.

As he gazed down at them, unable to tear his eyes away, he could feel his heart overflowing with so much love, and he found himself marvelling at how far he had come from the man he had once been, the man who'd married his wife without knowing how madly in love with her he was.

He had changed so much, and it was all because of Rae, he thought with a tender glance at her resting form. Because of her, he had learned to accept himself, to make his peace with the past and seize the future. Because of her, he felt safe, waking each morning without a single doubt in his heart or mind that he was loved, that he had *always* been loved, even if he hadn't been able to see it, and would continue to be for the rest of his days, and he never allowed a day to pass without making sure that Rae knew exactly the same thing.

* * * * *

Did this Rosie Maxwell story have you enthralled?
Then you're sure to adore her
previous book for Presents!

An Heir for the Vengeful Billionaire

Available now!

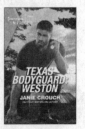